BOOK I, THE DRIEL TRILOGY

Enlightenment

{ LIZ KEEL }

Fire Quill Publishing
www.firequillpublishing.com
Copyright ©Liz Keel 2016
All rights reserved, including the right of reproduction in whole or in part
in any form.
All graphics and text associated with Fire Quill Publishing.
Formatting by www.firequillpublishing.com
Manufactured in South Africa and the USA
First Fire Quill publishing edition April 2016

ISBN-10: 0-9969748-7-3

ISBN-13: 978-0-9969748-7-5

DEDICATION

To Noah and Olivia,
for all the love and joy you bring to my life.

Acknowledgments

To my husband Richard – for all your support including finding those extra pockets of time for me to write whilst you looked after the children.

My friends and family – for being my eternal cheerleaders, giving me words of encouragement when I needed them the most.

Denise and Steph – for giving me the support and encouragement to help me realise my dream.

The fantastic team at Fire Quill Publishing – I truly couldn't have asked for any more support or encouragement from you all. You answered my endless questions with patience and always listened to what I had to say.

Lastly and most importantly - to you, the readers, for choosing to read my story, I hope you enjoy it.

CONTENT

"There are things known and things unknown, and in between are the doors of perception."

-Aldous Huxley

ONE

THE NIGHTMARE

"No!" I screamed. It had happened again. This was the fourth night in a row I had woken up with a start, beads of sweat dampening my forehead and a sick feeling swirling in my stomach. Rubbing my face whilst trying to sit up I thought back to the same terrifying dream that had been haunting me for weeks now. Not that I expected it to be any other way. I mean, watching your parents die in a car crash will have that effect on you. The difference was that I was supposed to have died. I know it sounds crazy but there was no way I should have survived that; yet I had, and I was sure that the only reason I was still alive was because of the bright light that had emanated from my body.

We were supposed to have been setting off on a three-month expedition around India, but only got as far as our local town in Montana before it happened. One minute I was sitting in the back of the car fiddling with my iPod and the next second I'd heard Mom screaming. I'd looked up just in time to see a car skidding along on the road before it hit us side-on, flipping us into a ditch. Even now the fear I'd felt at the time – the fear of what was to come – still swallows me whole. Time had seemed to slow down as I had watched my mom and dad being thrown around as the car had turned upside down. Our screams had been overwhelming and I'd been reaching my breaking point, when suddenly all went silent and I had been engulfed in a bright, orange glow that had blinded me. Everything after that was hazy. I remember smacking my head on the window, which had been followed by an unbearable pain that had made my skull feel as though it would explode. I put my hand to my forehead, feeling a warm and sticky liquid trickling down the side of my face. Putting my hand out in front of me, I saw it was blood, but my fuzzy brain couldn't comprehend what I was seeing. It was at that point black spots started to creep into my vision, making everything seem blurry. Then, however much I tried to stay awake, the darkness won and I slipped out of consciousness.

I awoke to an incessant bleeping and hushed whispers of 'So young' and 'Such a shame' and it was at that point I knew both of my parents were dead. Upon opening my eyes, a numb feeling began to take over as I realised I was in the local hospital with doctors giving me sympathetic looks and calling me sweetie whilst a nurse asked me who they should contact. That was an easy answer: no one. My parents had both been only children and their parents, my grandparents, had died when they were young. There was no one else.

A couple of hours later Eli turned up with his family. Who's Eli? Explaining him isn't exactly one of the easiest things to do, as our relationship was complicated to say the least. Foremost, he's my best friend, even with his over-protective nature, which I think stems from his need to look out for me, kind of like how I imagined a brother would for a sister. This would make sense as I've always been really close to his family, who seem to have been in my life for forever. Yes, it was helped by the fact they lived in the same neighbourhood as us and that he went to the same high school as me; but more than that Eli seems to have been there at all my major life events. From losing my first tooth, to falling off my bike and then taking me for walks in the forest when I needed the company, he's always been there, someone I could rely on.

And again on this eventful day, he turned up knowing exactly what I needed: for someone not to say anything, but instead just to sit with me. He completely ignored his mother's sobs as he only had eyes for me, walking quickly over to my bed and wrapping his arms around me. He pulled me onto his lap and once again I seemed to fit perfectly as he cocooned me, wrapping his arms around my back, his warmth spreading through me like a drug. We were both seniors but he looked older, probably due to the growth spurt he had had over the summer. At six foot one he was a whole seven inches taller than me and had these tanned muscular arms that were freakishly strong, probably due to his part-time job as a labourer on the local farm. His dark blond hair spent most of the time being brushed back from his forehead, as it always fell into his eyes, but it always really suited him that way. One of the things I loved most about him were his eyes, which sparkled different shades of emerald green and I swear just looking at them let me know how he was feeling. On that day they had been a dull green.

I know the way I'm describing him might make you wonder why I'm not talking about him as something more than just a friend, but that's the complicated part. You see, my feelings for him are purely platonic, but I don't think he feels the same. The way Eli looks at me sometimes...the subtle hints...the way he grabs my hand and won't let go, I think he wants something more and I'm not sure what to do about it. And however selfish this might sound, I need him in my life and can't mess up our friendship, even to see if there could possibly be something more to our relationship. What if it all went wrong?

"Hey Thea," Eli had whispered into my ear. "Mom says that when you're discharged you're coming home with us, period. No arguing." I'd squeezed him back, gratefully burying my face in the crook of his neck, unable to communicate how much he and his family meant to me. At least they would be able to keep the loneliness at bay.

We sat like that for ages, me just breathing in his woody, musky smell, wondering how I was meant to function again. He twisted strands of my dark brown hair around his fingers and occasionally stroked his thumb along the side of my chin in a soothing manner. I could hear his mother and father in deep discussions with the police officers, and heard them say it was a miracle I was alive. Tell me about it. The only other person who had been around was Eli's four-year-old sister Leela, who kept coming up with big, round, sad eyes, patting me on the leg whilst trying to get me to take Buggles, her much loved toy rabbit. She had known something was wrong and had tried her hardest to fix it in the only way she knew how.

That was four months ago, and although I've spent most of my time since then feeling numb and totally lost, I have begun to smile again and do normal things like getting up in the morning and going to school. If only these dreams would go away. There was nothing I could do about what had happened, but still my brain was making me re-play it over and over again. However, this latest dream was different.

Whenever I had dreamt about the crash, before the part where the orange glow appeared, I could see the faces of the bystanders with their horrified looks as we began to tip over. But this last time there was another face of a man who looked at me – and I mean really looked at me – as though he knew me. For some reason his eyes glowed with an intense ferocity and the sneer on his face only added to the anger that seemed to radiate off him. I couldn't work out what I had ever done to him, or why I hadn't seen him in my dreams before.

I sighed and looked at the clock, which read five a.m. Not wanting to wake Eli or his family I dressed quickly, got into my trainers and, with iPod in hand, left to go for a jog. It felt so good running and I always ended up in the same place – the forest by my old house. Being around nature felt so therapeutic, like I could actually absorb the energy around me. Weird, huh?! Today was no different as the early morning mist cloaked around me, like it was hugging me. Every now and then rays of morning light would shine in between the trees, warming my face. No one else was around, which was bliss, and I pushed myself even harder as though running faster would make the dream go away.

I wasn't surprised when sometime later Eli found me sitting against the rock at our usual spot overlooking the stream. I often sat here when I wanted to think. It was so peaceful, almost magical.

"Couldn't sleep?" he asked.

I nodded. "I dreamt about it again." 'It' was something we didn't often mention. However hard he had tried, I just couldn't come to terms with what had been termed the 'tragic accident' myself. Eli had tried everything, from gently cajoling me to actually shaking me one day, getting so frustrated that I wasn't letting it out. But what was there to let out? I was totally numb inside. Even his mom had tried to get me to talk and when that didn't work, she felt it would be best if I spoke to the school counsellor, but what was the point? I mean, they were dead. I decided not to tell Eli about the man who had suddenly appeared in my latest dream, as it sounded crazy.

"You know, it will get easier," he sighed. "It just takes time and..." he paused, getting something out of his pocket, "...a Twizzler." He smiled, eyes twinkling as he handed me the much loved candy. When he looked at me like he was doing right now, with my favourite cheeky grin, I couldn't help but go all warm and fuzzy inside. He leaned in closer, his breathing tickling the back of my neck. I changed the subject, not sure where this was going.

"One day of freedom left before the new semester starts," I groaned. "Do you think Mr Gregson is going to be as obnoxious as always?"

"Probably." Eli laughed. "At least this year we are in the same homeroom and have most of our classes together."

I murmured in agreement, relieved that once again he would be there, a constant presence. Sometimes it really did feel like he was my own personal guardian.

TWO

THE AMBUSH

The shaking wouldn't stop and my whole body seemed to react to what I had re-lived...again. This time the man started walking towards me whilst I was trapped in the car, angrily shouting a message he was adamant I was going to hear. I did.

I knew I must have woken someone up this time as my screams continued to ring out much longer than normal. Eli was the first in and padded softly over to my bed, a sympathetic look on his face. Just as he sat down, his mom popped her head around the door. "All okay?" she asked.

I nodded in answer. "Sorry, I didn't mean to wake you... I just...." I stopped, shrugging helplessly, feeling embarrassed.

"It's okay, just let me know if you need anything," she said, sharing a look with Eli as she left.

"So the same again?" he asked.

"Yes, but there's more," I whispered apprehensively as I crawled into his lap. Hoping he wouldn't think I was crazy, I told him about the man in the dream. I waited as he sat there thoughtfully rubbing the morning stubble that had appeared on his chin.

"Tell me again what he said."

"That I had ruined everything and I was still going to die," I said, my breath coming out in short gasps. I jumped up and began pacing around the room. "It seemed so real and I can't shake this feeling that I know him from somewhere, or that I've met him before."

As I stared distractedly out of the window into the pitch black night, I felt Eli's arms come around me in a warm embrace. My shoulders sagged. His touch had the calming effect I needed and I let him lead me back to bed. Once again I snuggled into him and began to breathe more normally.

"Thea, it's going to be okay, I know it may not seem it, but it will. I'm here for you, I...." And then he stopped. I felt like I knew what he was going to say and didn't know if I could handle that right now, so I turned and gave him a weak smile, quickly thanking him before he could finish his sentence.

"It's the first day of school tomorrow so we better get some sleep," Eli replied, returning my smile. "Good night," he said, kissing my forehead before he left.

Leela stared at me wistfully over the breakfast table. "But I wanna come," she sniffed. "So does Buggles, don't you?" she said, making the rabbit's head bounce up and down.

"Not long until it's your turn," her dad said, ruffling her hair as he walked by.

"Ready?" Eli called to me as he came down the stairs.

"Ready as I'll ever be," I laughed and grabbed my bag, heading for the door.

"Have a good day!" Mrs Thompson said, kissing us both on the cheek, "and be safe," she continued, giving Eli a meaningful look. I gave him a puzzled glance as she turned away: it was only school, after all. But he just shrugged and walked down the pathway with me in tow.

It was about a fifteen-minute walk to our bus stop down a long winding track, past the forest I loved so much. We started off in silence, both caught up in our own thoughts, and it wasn't until we were at the turnpike that I got the uneasy feeling we were being watched. I glanced into the forest, trying to see if there was anything out of place, but all I was greeted with was the dense undergrowth. I think Eli noticed it too because he seemed to tense up, and put his arm protectively around me, which brought me to a stop.

In the next instant, three men dressed in black jumped out from the bushes. Two of them went straight for me whilst the third put out his hands towards Eli. Somehow, without even touching him, he managed to throw Eli backwards about ten feet, where he hit the floor and skidded to a halt. My screams for help were drowned out when one of the attackers clamped a cold, calloused hand over my mouth. I bit down hard, which elicited a shout in a foreign-sounding language. Luckily this was enough for him to release me, and I felt some sort of inner victory knowing that I had managed to hurt him, even if it was only just a little bit.

I struggled to break free when suddenly he twisted

my arm over my head and kicked me in the back. I fell forward, landing heavily on the gravel path, smacking my head in the process. A sharp pain seared through my body and I screamed in agony. Eli turned towards me, a look of desperation on his face as he tried to get to me, but he was still preoccupied with his own attacker.

My eyesight dimmed and dizziness began to set in. Both my attackers decided to turn me over to face them, towering over me. The searing pain increased tenfold from the movement, and I narrowed it down to my ribs and left wrist, as well as the throbbing in my head. Something was definitely broken and the pain was making me feel sick.

Glancing up at Eli, I realised he was shouting words in a kind of musical and otherworldly tone, none of which made any sense to me, and that's when I knew I must have hit my head hard. As everything began to go fuzzy, I looked up at the one binding my hands with tape and gasped. "No..." I stammered, "...you're not real, who are you?!"

Staring inches away from my face with the same fixed sneer was the man from my dreams. The one who wanted me dead.

Then the panic really began to set in. I could feel it building up slowly at first and then swallowing me whole, engulfing me completely. At the same time, all around me was the same orange glow I had seen in the car accident. It was coming from my hands and surrounded my whole body as though it wanted to create a protective shell around me. Bizarrely, the light didn't stop just at me, it went around Eli as well. I couldn't comprehend how this was happening. I mean, it's not every day humans do what I was currently doing. Trying not to have a total freak out, I concentrated on the fact that whatever was going on would hopefully mean Eli and I would get out of this situation in one piece.

Becoming stronger, the light turned into flames, and although I somehow knew it wouldn't harm us, I couldn't stop the feeling of horror coursing through me. What was going on? Our attackers, suddenly seeing this turn of events, began to back away, which gave Eli much needed time to fight back and take control as he took on all three at once. I didn't realise until now how similar the three of them looked. All were grotesque and slightly disfigured. Evil seemed to ooze out of their pores, and hung in darkness around them. They were so dirty, and wore an odd mixture of clothes, as though they were trying to fit in but were failing miserably.

Gusts of wind, like mini tornados, began swirling in a growing vortex as they shot out from Eli's hands, smacking forcefully into our attackers who screamed before they bent over double and fell to the floor, unmoving. Eli staggered over to me. "It's okay, you can stop now, they won't harm us," he gasped, as I fought for control over whatever it was I had done. It was only when I knew the threat had passed that the glow began to fade from my hands and then everything went blank.

THREE

MY LIFE IN A NUTSHELL...WHO KNEW?

I groaned, feeling like I had the worst headache ever. Opening my eyes I saw Eli peering down at me with a concerned look on his face. "You've got a nasty cut on your head," he said, applying the gentlest of pressure so as not to hurt me. "You've also got a broken rib and have sprained your wrist," he continued matter-of-factly, whilst a burning emotion shone through his eyes. As he was talking I realised he was finishing wrapping a tight bandage around my chest. I tried to hide my embarrassment when I realised he had full view of my bra and stomach, as my shirt had been pulled open whilst he worked.

"How are you feeling?" Eli asked, totally engrossed

in what he was doing and unaware of my inner turmoil.

"Fine…actually great!" I croaked as I tried to stand up. Bad idea: the world started spinning.

"Whoa," he said. "You're okay, we're safe, but we've gotta keep moving…here, lean on me." He gently bent down and put his arm around my waist. "I think they're going to come back."

"How do you know?" I started and then began to realise something. "Eli, this is going to sound crazy, but the guy who tried to tie me up was the one from my dream. He was the guy who wanted me dead." The panic began to spread as I ran my fingers through my hair, trying to understand what the hell had just happened.

"Not now, okay? Come on, we have to go!" he said firmly. Seeing my overwhelming fear, he gently put his hands around my face and stared into my blue eyes. "I will explain all of this to you soon, I promise." His determined look gave me some hope we would get out of this alive.

He held onto my face until he knew I was okay and had stopped freaking out. "I'm not going to let anything happen to you, I haven't so far," he said softly, and with that we started to move – as much as my body would let me.

"Wait, where are we going?" I started.

"Not back to the house, it's not safe, into the forest…NOW!"

Eli began running, half dragging me as he went, just as we heard angry shouts behind us. Knowing if we didn't move quickly we would be in trouble, it was all I could do to keep up with his relentless pace and follow.

We seemed to go deeper and deeper into the undergrowth, and with everything that had happened to me it wasn't long before I began to struggle. Feeling light-headed, I leaned further onto Eli as my breath began to come out in short gasps. Soon I had no idea where we were.

Realising I was getting worse, Eli gently pulled me down to lean against a tree. He inspected my injuries as I tried to get my breath. I'd had enough.

"Stop! You need to tell me what's going on," I wheezed out as I started trembling, suddenly feeling as if I was in real danger. "And why didn't you seem surprised to see those…creatures?"

He let out a deep breath. "Wait here," he commanded, frustration etched over his face. "I will explain, but first I need to check we've lost them," he said, before backtracking along the route we'd just come.

Only a few minutes had passed before Eli returned, and after nodding in reassurance at my questioning look as to whether we were in the clear, he sat down.

Giving me a guarded look, he was obviously trying to find the right words before he spoke. "This wasn't how I planned on telling you, but now I have no choice. What I'm going to say will change your life forever and you must know I haven't told you any of this before now because your safety is paramount and I was trying to protect you," he said, pleading for me to understand.

Ok, I wasn't expecting that. Propping myself up as best I could, I tried to prepare myself for what he was going to say next, and hugged my arms around myself protectively.

"Thea, you aren't actually human, you're an Elf; and

not just any Elf, but one with royal blood in you."

It was only because of how serious he looked that I didn't start laughing. I held my breath, waiting for him to continue.

"When you were just a baby, our kingdom, Aroben, was fighting over who should rule – the royal blood line or the Elf Council. At the time it was the king and queen who were in control and they were much loved by Elves across the land. They sought guidance from the Elf Council, in particular about elemental debates."

Seeing my confused look, he continued, "You see, an Elf is gifted by the goddess Elebrin with an element when they are born. They have an affiliation to either earth, air, fire, water, or in rare cases spirit. In order that Elves of all elements have a say in the running of the land, each element has a representative on the Council. It is their job to liaise with the king and queen over matters across the land."

Eli sighed, lost in thought.

"What went wrong?" I asked, entranced by what he was saying, but not believing a word of it.

"Minen, the Council Elder Principal who presided over the other five Elders, felt some elements shouldn't be as powerful as others, and consequently he wanted this to be reflected in the amount of status and power they could each have on the Council. You can imagine how that was received," Eli said, raising his eyebrows at me.

"Well, if people thought he was crazy why didn't they just get rid of him?" I asked, getting more and more caught up in this fantasy he was weaving.

"The king and queen tried, especially with all the civil unrest that was beginning to creep across the land, but Minen had powerful allies who helped him with his cause. He even tried to initiate a vote of no confidence, but fortunately the majority of Aroben still supported the monarchy."

Listening to Eli and seeing his dejected face, I knew what was coming next.

"War broke out, two opposing sides forming quickly. Elves affiliated with fire sided with Minen as he said their element was the most powerful. The water and air Elves were split as to where their loyalties lay, but fortunately for us the majority sided with the king and queen. Earth Elves, who were considered to have the weakest element under Minen's crazy ideals, began to go into hiding, worried about what the consequences would be for them if he actually came to power. The fifth elementals, those who could control spirit, were so few in number that they kept to themselves and tried not to get too involved. Many were worried though that Minen might start trying to use them for his own means due to their uncommon powers.

"Even with us having the majority on our side, after many months no one gained the upper hand and many lives were lost due to the constant fighting. Minen, seeing he was unlikely to win, began to turn to desperate measures and sought the help of the Goblins, a species disliked by many all over Faery. The Goblins' greed for precious jewels, of which we have many, meant they could easily be bought and with their help Minen and his followers attacked the palace one night. The result was disastrous: the king and queen were killed, which left the kingdom in a precarious situation as to who would be left to lead us in the fight."

Turning to look at me, he continued. "Thea...the king and queen were your real parents."

He stopped, assessing how I was holding up. Rolling my eyes in response, I wasn't quite sure why he was still continuing with this farcical story. I mean, yes those men who attacked me did seem otherworldly, but it didn't mean any of this was true, and trying to make out my parents were the king and queen from another realm was just ridiculous, as well as being completely insensitive. It wasn't that long ago I'd lost them, and now he was making out they weren't even my real parents.

"Eli, enough of this already. I know you're trying to distract me and take my mind off what's happened, but stop with this story. It's not funny," I finished, shoving him slightly, trying to get him to realise I was beginning to get pissed. It was like he was losing the plot. Maybe he had hit his head harder than I'd thought.

He grabbed my hand and began rubbing it soothingly, finally seeing I had a big problem with what he was saying. "Thea, I'm not making this up, however far-fetched it might seem. This story is true. I need you to understand what's going on, and the sooner the better. We don't have much time..." He trailed off before watching me hesitantly to see if I'd continue to listen.

"When we realised what had happened, and the danger your life was in as next in-line for the throne, we acted quickly. Not all the members on the Council were corrupt and power-hungry. Talawen, leader of the Spirit Elves, was a good friend of your family and sent you into the human world thinking you would be safe there. The people you thought of as your parents were actually members of the Thill guard, an elite group of Elves who serve the throne. I was also assigned to guard you.

"For many years whilst you were growing up all seemed well. The amount of protections we had placed on you and the house played an important part in this. Then seven months ago, when you turned seventeen, Minen succeeded in tracking you and tried to have you killed in that car accident. However, all it achieved was the death of Erwin and Tanidur, your guardians. No one knows how you survived, but after seeing how you protected yourself when we were under attack today, I'm thinking there is more to your elemental magic than meets the eye."

"Hang on a minute!" I snorted, seeing a flaw in this explanation of his. How could he have been my guard all this time when he was just seventeen like me? Or was he?

Swallowing a whole lot of emotion, I tried to ask the next question with more calm than I felt.

"How old are you?"

Eli gave me a cautious look, like he knew I was going to freak.

"One hundred and fourteen."

"Oh," was all I could reply at first, my head reeling from his answer. I had always felt Eli looked and acted older than he seemed, and now I knew why.

"So if you're 114, why do you look like you do?" I said, throwing my arms out in disbelief. "I mean…do all Elves look freakishly young or something?! And why did you look the same age as me whilst we were growing up?"

"Ok, I can see your point," Eli replied, putting his hands out in a placating gesture. "This might be hard to believe but the world I – we – come from isn't like the human realm. To answer your first question, I look like I do, and by that I mean like someone around twenty who's very sexy and handsome," he smirked, "because all Elves do. We stop aging at the same rate as humans when we turn twenty-one and from then on our aging happens at a very slow rate. You'll be pleased to know these good looks will last for a long time to come, especially as we usually live for a thousand years, give or take. In Aroben I'm still considered young!

"Answering your second question, whilst you were growing up I was enchanted to appear your age when around you or any other humans. Then when I turned 'seventeen,'" Eli continued, using air quotes to illustrate his point, "the enchantment was broken, so I now look like my regular, charming self."

Eli grinned at my incredulous look and I stood up, ready to get away from this crackpot. Where was my best friend and who was this nutter? Resting my arm protectively over my ribs, I watched him warily as he too rose, watching me like I was some sort of flighty animal about to take off.

"Eli, stop this!" I snapped, the pain I was in fuelling my anger. "You're either insane or incredibly insensitive. What makes you think I want to hear this bunch of crap after everything I've been through? My parents died, Eli, they died. Not in some other crazy, made-up kingdom, but here in the human realm where you and I belong. Don't you dare say they didn't." I trembled, turning away from him as angry, hot tears began to leak down my face. Brushing them away, my frustration began to build, and at that moment I'd rather have been anywhere than there.

"Thea..." he started in response, reaching out tentatively to grab a hold of my hand.

Refusing to turn around, I waited for him to apologise.

"Thea..." Eli started again, trying to pull on my hand so I'd face him.

"No Eli, don't." I started to sob as my body betrayed me, wanting to seek his comfort whilst my head was still so pissed at him. "You don't get to treat me this way, you need to stop now or I'm going," I finished, using the only threat I knew would work to make him realise how deadly serious I was. There was no way he'd want me leaving to venture off on my own without him.

"Thea," he started a third time, his voice cracking as it matched the emotions I was feeling inside. "I'm not lying, I'm not," he insisted again, seeing I was about to interrupt him. "I know I'm hurting you, but I don't have any other choice. There is only one option open to us now, and that's to head home...your Elven home. You'll be safe there, there will be more of us to protect you," he explained, hoping the matter of my safety would help me see reason.

Feeling utterly confused, I sighed and closed my eyes, trying to digest his latest revelations. Seeing me begin to soften, he continued on with the story, as though he was trying to get it all out before I refused to listen to him anymore. It still didn't mean I was beginning to believe him.

"When we realised Minen knew where you were, Erwin contacted Talawen, who felt you would be safer if you returned home to Aroben. You would soon be entering the age of enlightenment, when you would become one with your element, and this normally happens when you're seventeen," he said, and it was at that moment a niggly thought crept into my head.

What had made me produce those flames earlier? Surely I hadn't really used fire to protect myself?

"When you were to return, Talawen wanted you to start your training in secret so that when the time was right we could show you to the kingdom and claim control again."

"Training for what?" I asked, becoming completely distracted by the thoughts churning through my head.

"All Elves learn archery, defence, including how to fight with weapons, our history and their role in our future. To become enlightened, you also receive training in how to harness the magical qualities of your element. It can take an Elf years to train, and becoming enlightened is a condition you must meet before you can become queen, let alone because you will need these skills to go up against Minen."

Eli sighed, running his hands distractedly through his hair, making it look even more dishevelled.

"That was the plan anyway. The portal to get back to the otherworld was actually supposed to open up for us tomorrow, not far from here."

I wasn't sure if this was some horrible drawn-out prank or not, but I was overwhelmed by the sudden pressure pulsing through my body as I realised how important I possibly was to so many people, and I felt sick to my stomach. Surely this story wasn't real? I wasn't special, and certainly didn't feel like I was going to have an affiliation with a particular element. What would happen then? Yes, I knew that when close to nature I felt like I was able to absorb its energy, which would kind of make sense if I believed what Eli was saying, but no way could I do anything special enough to use in a fight to save an entire kingdom.

"You are quite unique, Thea," Eli said as though he

could tell what I was thinking. "And I'm not going anywhere. You don't have to face this on your own," he finished, staring at me with so much love in his eyes.

Would Eli really play such an elaborate joke on me? I was certain he wouldn't, but this story seemed far too strange to be true. Regardless, Eli was very important to me and if what he said was true, then I'd need him now, more than ever.

Sitting back down again, I rested my head on his shoulder and sighed, exhaustion seeping through me. My wrist was on fire and its steady throb seemed to match the drumming that was pounding away in my head, both a very realistic reminder of what had happened a few hours before.

Sometime later I realised I must have fallen asleep, as I woke up with my head lying in Eli's lap. The warmth from his body felt good and seemed to give me some strength. I turned to look up at his face, to see his intense gaze returned right back at me.

"So what now?" I asked, holding my breath and getting lost in the emotion behind his eyes.

"We fight."

FOUR

Goodbye Human World, Hello Faery

"Come on, not much further now," Eli said, as he hurried on ahead.

Okay, I'm not normally grumpy, but really, we had been travelling for most of the night, my whole body ached and I wasn't quite sure how Eli knew where we were heading as everything looked the same. The only consolation was now that the sun was beginning to rise, it made it easier to miss the tree roots that were causing me to trip up every couple of minutes, and we seemed to have completely lost our attackers.

I continued to mutter to myself, grumbling as we journeyed to what must have been the centre of the forest. As my home was in Montana, I knew we could keep walking in this particular forest for days before we met anyone.

After a while, the trees around us became denser with every step, and even in my exhausted state I could sense the change around us as birds stopped tweeting and we were met with complete silence, which was only broken by our movements when we stepped over the occasional log or snapped a branch or twig. I could also sense a strong energy around us and knew we must be getting close to the portal. An hour or so later we entered a clearing that had a circular patch of grass in the middle and not much else. Eli knelt down and put his hands – palms out – towards a tree, which had to be at least a thousand years old judging by how tall and wide it was. The knotted roots alone came up to my thigh and twisted in all directions. As I began to concentrate on what he was doing, I saw his hands glow brightly and the tree responded. At first it looked like it was shimmering, and then this faded completely, leaving in its place an entrance that I knew would lead to Faery. I stopped, trying to take in this moment, knowing I would be leaving my old life, everything, behind. I couldn't help the freak out that was beginning to take over. This was just too much. Eli was telling the truth. I really was an Elf from another realm! What the hell?

It took me a moment to realise Eli had bent me over slightly and was rubbing my back as he tried to slow my breathing. Everything took on a fuzzy look as I became light-headed and I clasped on tightly to Eli's hands just to stop the shaking getting worse. He turned to look at me and nodded his head, meaning for me to come forward, and as I took a deep breath, the thought of going into a land that only a day ago I had never heard of seemed ridiculous, especially since my life would be in even more danger. Swallowing that fear, I stepped through.

It took me a few moments to gauge my first impressions of Faery. At first it didn't seem that different to Montana. In fact, I did wonder if I really had stepped into another realm, but then, the more I looked at what I was seeing, the more the subtle differences became apparent. Taking off my cardigan, I realised the climate was just that bit warmer, a couple of degrees I'd say, possibly due to the fact that there were two – yes, two – suns shining down on me. Huge exotic looking flowers filled the ground on every side, fighting for space, like they were trying to get my attention, and I realised that maybe they were. You see, it felt like they were trying to project their energy into me as feelings of nostalgia hit me, remembering I would often feel this way on my runs back in the human realm. However, the big difference was that the level of energy I was able to absorb from the nature here was so much greater. This, coupled with a sense of belonging, finally made me realise how much I had been lied to by the one person who meant so much, and a new wave of anger coursed through me as I finally snapped.

"How could you?" I shouted furiously. "You have been lying to me my entire life. I trusted you! I believed in you!!" I continued, my voice rising higher and higher in pitch. "This is something you should have told me ages ago, Eli. I had a right to know everything, that I'm an Elf, and a queen!" I yelled now, as he looked on guiltily. "How am I supposed to process all of this? How am I supposed to handle everything that's still to come? I trusted you. You were my best friend…" I growled, wanting to cause him physical pain of the worst kind.

"I still am," he replied gently, bravely coming up to stand next to me, even with the look of murder I was giving him. "Thea, I truly am sorry, but I had my orders, I wasn't allowed to tell you until it was time to return. You mean everything to me, you know that," he cajoled, and, seeing my temper was beginning to simmer, he redirected the conversation back to the here and now.

"The Elf Kingdom, Aroben, is a day's journey this way," he said, pointing towards a clearing, "...and in about half a day's travel the Thill guard will be meeting us."

As we set off at a steady pace, resigned to even more travelling, I began to think further about my relationship with Eli. I hadn't exactly been close like this with any other guy before. Don't get me wrong, I'd had a couple of boyfriends, but not ones that seemed to know everything about me like he did. Yes of course I was irritated with him for not telling me my whole life had been a lie, but now the even bigger problem I faced was whether the feelings I was picking up from him meant he wanted to be with me for me, or because he felt I needed protecting out of some sense of duty. Confusing or what? Alongside this I still hadn't sorted out if he did want to be with me, whether I would come to want the same.

Giving him a side-glance, he caught my eye and grinned. He already seemed much more relaxed here than back in the human world.

"So there are lots of things about you I obviously don't know," I began, raising my eyebrows. Eli looked suitably sheepish as I continued. "Why were you picked as my babysitter?"

"Don't see it like that," he urged. "I was chosen as

I'm part of the Thill guard whose role in life is to protect and serve the royal family, of which you are now the most important member. Well...the only member." He paused before continuing.

"I should explain that after the death of your parents, Minen took over as king and has maintained a cruel and tyrannical regime for sixteen years now, which makes my job as protector to you, as our princess, even more important. The Earth Elves in particular have been treated terribly and have few rights in our society. Even Erwin, the Earth Council Elder, realises he is just a figurehead with no actual power."

Eli smiled at me, knowing I would start objecting to being called a princess even if it was true.

"It is a great honour to be part of the Thills and to be asked to guard you," he continued. "I knew that although I'd be leaving my family behind, keeping you alive to help save our kingdom was the most important role I could fulfil.

"I was chosen with Erwin and Tanidur, as well as my make believe 'human' family, to keep you safe at all costs. For years it was easy to forget my mission and slip into human life. I'm sorry, Thea. Because I let you down, letting Minen come so close to killing you is my fault and now you need even greater protection, and however much I wish I could, I now can't do that on my own," he muttered, looking pained by his own words.

I could see the inner turmoil Eli was experiencing and this brought on another round of questions.

"What's it like in Aroben at the moment? I mean...why hasn't anyone else tried to overthrow Minen?"

"It's not that simple," he started. "Law states that either the royal line or Council may permit a change to how things are run, but as the kingdom believes all members of the royal family including yourself were killed, Minen as the head of the Council was the only option we had. Of course he wasn't going to implement change to the running of Aroben as he has everything he wants right at his fingertips. His power runs deep, and, with strong allies, we haven't had any choice but to follow his leadership.

"Life in Aroben is not safe and I have heard word recently of Earth Elves disappearing. No one knows where they have been taken, but we suspect Minen is behind it. Everyone is just turning a blind eye to all his treachery."

Oh great, this was getting even better. I was dreading the answer to my next question.

"How am I supposed to behave in front of him when he finds out I'm back? Has he ever been tried for what he did to my parents?"

"What Minen did to your parents has never been proven, and over the years the Elves have just believed his story that Trolls came in and wreaked havoc in the palace and the king's and queen's deaths were the tragic result. However, there are those who still know the true story. This therefore puts you in a difficult situation, as you will not be able to accuse Minen of anything. The easiest way to overthrow him is to take your place as queen, which you are entitled to. You will need to remain civil towards him and bite your tongue, as he still influences many who hold great power."

I snorted, trying to process this ridiculous situation I now faced, let alone now having to come to terms with the fact that Trolls were actually real. After a few moments of silence, I changed to a lighter topic.

"Is your family still in Aroben? Do they know you're coming back?"

"Yes, my mother, father and sister Kayla live here, and no, they don't know I'm coming back."

"Do they look like you?" I enquired, and as an afterthought said, "I thought Elves had pointed ears?!"

Eli chuckled. "We do, and so do you, but it's the magical qualities of Aroben that give us our pointed ears, along with a powerful link to our element."

Just then he grabbed me and pulled me behind him so I was out of sight of whatever was ahead of us. He tensed, ready, as a sense of dread filled me. Surely we could not be facing more danger already? Looking around, I realised his tall frame meant the only thing I could see was the undergrowth surrounding me, leafy green trees and some bizarre looking purple flowers covered in spikes. Then moments later I heard the rustling that had obviously set him on alert, and I leaned around him. Eight Elves all in the same black outfit with a brown and silver tunic over the top walked through the undergrowth. They had bows strapped to their backs and daggers resting against each hip, and boy, did they look intimidating. All rivalled Eli in height and wore stoic expressions; however, one stood out from the rest – the one at the front – as he stepped forward, allowing me to see him more clearly in all his glory. My heart nearly stopped as I stared at this being that radiated magnificence and perfection.

Eli's stance began to relax and he stepped forward with an air of familiarity to meet the Elf I had been staring at. Both made a strange gesture at each other that I could only assume was a greeting. Looking oddly formal, they placed a fist over their hearts whilst facing each other.

"Isaac! How are you?" Eli said, giving him a warm smile.

"Eli." Isaac nodded back, gracing him with a similar smile before turning his gaze upon me. The intense, assessing look he gave as he searched my face was nothing short of hot and had me wanting to melt in a puddle on the floor. I was shocked by my body's response to him. All I wanted to do was to get closer to him, to mould my body against his. I had never met anyone who was able to evoke such strong feelings within me with just one look.

It felt like we were connected somehow and I stared on, becoming ensnared in those crystal blue eyes of his that seemed to pierce into my very soul. The more I stared, the more I had this feeling I had met him before but wasn't sure where. Like a distant memory that was fuzzy around the edges. But it didn't feel like just one fuzzy memory, it felt like he had been there in many key moments of my life, always on the periphery, but that was impossible, right?

My body continued to react to him, and the warmth that had started to spread through me heated up my core and I flushed, realising how turned on I was. I tried to clear the embarrassing thoughts that were beginning to creep into my head and let out a breath, trying to look as if he wasn't affecting me. However, turning to Eli, I saw him give me a funny look as though he knew something was up.

Watching Isaac watching me, I saw a flicker of raw emotion in his otherwise stoic expression that made me feel he had felt something too, like his soul was reconnecting with mine. And I knew in that moment that he knew me, really knew me. Yet why wasn't he acknowledging this – what we clearly were both feeling? Instead, glimpsing back in his eyes I noticed they now had a cold, steel-like edge to them, projecting the hardship and heartache he had obviously endured. Who was this guy, and what had happened to him? I shook my head, trying to snap out of the reverie I seemed to be in, and focused back on the here and now.

"We are well, thank you Eli," he started, still looking at me. "Although I am a little puzzled to see you so soon. We weren't expecting you until the rising of tomorrow's sun."

"Three Goblins sent by Minen attacked us as we were going to the humans' school. We were lucky to survive. If it hadn't been for Thea's..." He stopped, giving me a funny look as though he didn't want to share my glowing exploits just yet.

Using this time to roam over the rest of this god-like anomaly before me, I noticed he had a faint scar on his face that caught the sunlight every now and then, adding to his ethereal beauty. His chiselled jawline gave him a clean-cut appearance. However, his shaggy black hair seemed to be the contradiction as it took on a life of its own; I watched on as the wind caught his fringe and blew it in all directions, including his eyes. Oh, and yes, he had pointed ears.

Isaac was taller than Eli, but not by a lot, and that only added to the intimidating and slightly 'off' demeanour he was projecting. In fact, apart from that flicker of emotion when we'd first looked at each other, he now seemed closed and distant, to the point that I was surprised Eli responded to him with such warmth.

Still facing me, Isaac put his fist across his chest and bowed. "Thea-Driel, greetings to you. I am relieved to see that you are mostly unharmed from this encounter," he said with what sounded like a hint of agitation, as his gaze rested on my dishevelled and injured appearance.

"Th-thank you," I stammered, feeling embarrassed as not only he but all the guards were looking at me like I was some sort of precious jewel.

Interrupting the awkwardness that Eli could see I was experiencing, he addressed all the guards at once. "We better keep moving so we make Aroben before nightfall." And with that they seemed to move fluidly as one, surrounding Eli and myself, with Isaac taking the lead up front.

"Why did he call me Thea-Driel?" I whispered to Eli as he walked next to me.

"The last part of an Elf's name tells others about who they are, their past and family. It is also used as a formality when first greeting another Elf, especially one in the royal family. Driel is your family name and was the name your mother and father were known by," he said, a reminiscent expression on his face.

"What's yours?" I asked.

"Actually you've already heard it. It's Thill, Eli-Thill. I, and the other guard members, take on the name Thill once we become part of the elite guard, as we pledge our life to the throne and what it stands for. Our motto is *Eryuslian*, which roughly translates as 'to serve and protect'."

"What language is that? Do you all normally speak in another tongue?" I asked, presuming they must all just be speaking English for my benefit.

Isaac answered this time. "Actually we speak many

languages, including English, but Farun is our mother-tongue and has been passed down from generation to generation."

Digesting this latest piece of information, we stayed in this formation, with Eli and I in the middle surrounded by our guards for a further four hours, before we finally stopped for a rest. The further we journeyed, the more I began to notice other subtle differences in the nature around us. It was then that I also realised my movements were becoming easier, my ribs didn't ache so much and the visible bruises on my arms and legs were already turning a yellowy-green colour rather than the purple splotches I'd had only hours before.

"Your body is responding to the healing qualities the plants' energy is projecting into you. It's amazing, isn't it?" Eli stated, realising what I was thinking. I could only blink in response, definitely in awe of my new home. Looking out into the distance, my body continued to relax and heal, almost as though in its own way it was telling me I was safe here.

FIVE

AROBEN

Nearing the heart of Aroben raised another truckload of questions, but I held my tongue, preferring to ask Eli in private. I was also still very distracted by my feelings for Isaac.

After a while the land around us showed signs of being populated, and eventually we began to pass more and more Elves who stopped to stare at us - well, at me in particular - murmuring in excitement as though they knew who I was. It got worse as many then began bowing and greeting me like Isaac had, which made me feel even more awkward. I kept my head down and began to twist my hands together nervously.

Eli, seeing my reaction, struck up conversation to distract me. "There are many types of Elven homes, depending on the owner's elemental affinity. If you look up there you can make out those homes in the trees," he said, pointing to a wooded area nearby. "Homes up there are usually those of the Air Elves, whilst the Water Elves can be found residing near Lake Fallowen," Eli continued, pointing in a different direction. "That's where Janin and Taro live," he said, gesturing to two of the guards who turned to wink at me. I smiled back, wondering where I would feel most at home.

"The Earth Elves have built homes into the side of the mountains and the Fire Elves live deep underground where the temperature is a lot hotter," Janin joined in conversationally.

"What about the Spirit Elves?" I wondered, imagining them floating around carefree.

"Well, they don't have a particular preference, and as there aren't many, Spirit Elves are usually found either living with other elementals, or somewhere quiet and secluded," Taro replied.

"You will live in the palace, Thea. It was designed by incorporating materials from all the elements to show that we are equal and that all Elves are needed to work alongside one another in harmony...for the betterment of all," Eli announced.

"That's why it's a joke Minen lives here as well, as it goes against everything he believes. At least you'll never bump into him, the palace is so large, and with so many wings, you will only ever see him at Council meetings and functions," Janin explained.

Janin and Taro looked similar, although Taro's eyes were a lighter blue and his hair a slightly darker shade of blond. Both were very tall and looked like they could kick ass like Isaac and Eli.

As we took another path that led to the right, the

trees began to thin out and I found myself looking at the most beautiful building I had ever seen. Not that I had seen a palace in real life, only in pictures, but this one was beautiful.

Nestled into the side of a large hill, it was predominantly made out of stone with wooden arches, and the arch over the main doors had five symbols carved into it. Fountains were dotted around the gardens, which contained flowers of all colours and fragrances. At the back, you could just make out a lake. Eli told me it was Lake Fallowen. It seemed to stretch on forever until it eventually disappeared around a bend.

I was so relieved to have finally arrived and felt absolutely exhausted. All I wanted to do was have a shower and curl up in a nice warm bed, and hoped that would be possible without having to meet anyone new. Glancing my way Isaac must have realised how I felt as he spoke softly to me. "Thea-Driel, we will escort you to your room, which is ready for your arrival, and I will then inform Talawen you are here."

"He'll be most pleased to know you have arrived even though he wasn't expecting you this early," Eli stated. I just nodded, feeling too sleepy and overwhelmed to do much else.

The inside of the palace was just as beautiful and I knew that soon I would need to explore it in detail. As we walked through the different passages, I felt a bit silly having so many people taking me to my room, and upon entering, I was relieved that I could finally shut the door with them on the outside. Janin and Taro winked again before I closed them out, each grinning goodbye as they bowed before leaving. I knew I was going to have some fun with these two. Then, it was only Eli who remained with me.

"We made it," he smiled at me as though trying to ease some of the tension I was feeling. However, I could see the past few days had taken their toll on him as he suddenly looked away, but not before I saw the tears in his eyes. What we had been through had affected him more than he was willing to let on.

"So, rest tonight Thea," he began, wrapping his arms around me and cocooning me once again, making me feel safe and secure. "Tomorrow you will meet your nemesis, Minen. Isaac informed me he already knows you are here and has asked for you to meet him and the Elder court at nine a.m. but don't worry though, as both of us will meet with you beforehand to talk through strategy and discuss how you should deal with him and the other Elders who might be less than friendly towards you."

"Tell me more about Isaac," I blurted out, not wanting Eli to leave just yet. "I feel like I've met him before, he seems familiar. That sounds crazy right?" I hadn't meant to say the last part out loud; however, Eli's forced laugh and unwillingness to actually look at me made me think there was something more to this than met the eye.

"Don't be silly, Thea. Isaac's just got one of those faces."

That was hardly true.

"I can't work him out. You greeted him like he was an old friend but he didn't seem that warm or friendly to me," I continued.

"Isaac is a complicated character who has been through a lot. He's remained a good friend of mine and yes, he does have a heart," he smirked at me. "He's excellent at his job, which is why he is Head Thill. His fighting skills are renowned as being the best in Aroben and his passion and loyalty to the throne mean he is one of the most trusted guards around. Give him a chance," Eli urged.

If Eli only knew the way my body reacted to Isaac and the impure thoughts I continued to have, I didn't think he'd want me to give him a chance.

"How old is he?" I continued.

"Hundred and fifty-six, but don't let that fool you into thinking he is any wiser than me!" Eli laughed.

Suddenly a knock at the door had Eli looking all serious and guard-like again, until the door opened and he saw who it was. Then his face relaxed into a smile. The hug he gave the man standing before him was almost like a son embracing his father.

"Talawen, it's been far too long! How are you?!" Eli exclaimed before hugging him again.

"Need you really ask?" he replied, looking weary. "Minen has had you followed since you passed the 'Waterfall of Knowledge', but enough about that," he trailed off, patting Eli on the back. I could see this news worried Eli even though he tried hard to keep his face neutral.

"Talawen, let me reacquaint you with Thea," he said, changing the expression on his face and beckoning me forward. "Thea, this is Talawen, Council Elder Member for the Spirit Elves and someone who was a much loved friend of your parents."

As Talawen turned to face me, I found myself feeling awkward, and hugged myself, not sure what to do next. He clearly looked like he knew me, which would make sense if he was a friend of my parents, I guessed, but to me he was a complete stranger. I stepped forward and he shook my hand warmly before pulling me in for an embrace.

Just like the Thill guards, Talawen oozed authority and power. His grey eyes held a twinkle as he observed me fidgeting under his scrutiny, and his long, straight brown hair that reached his shoulders had streaks of grey in it. Judging on this fact alone, I guessed him to be much older than the Thills, as he looked to be in his mid-forties. Unlike the guards, he wore a light green cloak that reached the floor, and there was an emblem on the right side of the cloak above his chest with a symbol I didn't recognise.

"Thea-Driel, many moons have passed since we last met, and I fear that you may not remember me as you were just a child," he started fondly.

"You look well, even though I hear from Isaac you did not have the safest of journeys here. Thank the elements our prayers have been answered and you are able to stand before me again in our great kingdom."

I smiled and tried to suppress a yawn, which unfortunately they both saw.

"My apologies for not letting you rest, Thea. I will go now and see you in the Council meeting tomorrow. Rest assured that, whatever happens, there are many who are still true to you, princess. Do not be afraid." And with that he swept from the room.

Eli gave me a kiss on the forehead. "Sweet dreams," he whispered. "There are guards stationed outside your room, you'll be safe," he finished as he also took his leave.

Feeling like I could have passed out standing up, I walked over to the bed and lay down, falling asleep within a second of my head hitting the soft pillow.

SIX

THE COUNCIL OF ELDERS

The following morning I woke to find that somebody had placed clothes at the bottom of my bed whilst I had slept.

Relieved I wouldn't have to wear the same dirty, blood-encrusted outfit from the day before, I took a bath, grateful they also used this as a method to clean themselves, like in the human world.

Feeling much better, I dried off and took a closer look at the dress I had been left. It was beautiful. Dark green in colour, the material felt as though it was made with silk or something finer, and hugged me in all the right places. Putting it on I peeked in the mirror and was astonished to find my skin looking really clear and radiant somehow. Not just that, I realised I also felt different - healthier and stronger even than before I was injured. Even my rib and wrist felt back to normal, an incredible recovery rate. It was only twenty-four hours since the attack. I could see why Elves lived for such a long time, given the healing, magical qualities of the air in this realm.

Walking out into the corridor I found Janin and Taro on guard duty either side of my door. "Good morning, princess," they said, bowing in unison. Feeling unsure of what to do next I took a few tentative steps to the left, wondering if they would stop me.

Suddenly a voice behind me made me jump. "You're up, Thea-Driel. I trust you slept well," Isaac said as I turned around to look at him standing there in all his delicious glory. He did a double take as he looked at me in my dress and I saw that same heated gaze I'd witnessed briefly the day before. Feeling slightly awkward, I glanced down and took a deep breath before looking back up to see that his impassive look was already back in place. I wondered if maybe I was misreading the situation. Maybe it was all in my head. What with Eli's possible feelings towards me, I had enough to deal with without creating further drama.

"I am to escort you to breakfast and then take you on to the Council Elder Meeting."

"Th-thank you," I stammered, trying once again to ignore the way his eyes seemed to bore into me. He had to be one of the most handsome men I'd ever met, but I couldn't shake off this feeling that radiated off of him – that merely being in my presence frustrated him somehow.

We started walking along the pathway we had come down last night, along some stone steps and into a walled courtyard. I kept giving him a sideways glance, waiting for him to speak, but when he didn't I started up conversation instead, not being able to bear the silence any longer.

"So, do you know where Eli is? He said he would be meeting me," I squeaked, feeling like an idiot.

"Eli-Thill will be along shortly," he said, looking straight ahead. Suddenly feeling nervous due to who I was about to face, it felt like hundreds of butterflies were fluttering in my stomach and I wasn't sure how I was going to eat even though I was starving. The last thing I had eaten was breakfast, and that had been over twenty-four hours ago.

We walked into a welcoming dining room with a view overlooking the lake. Seeing lots of delicious fruit and bread on the table I walked over and grabbed an apple just as Eli appeared. The relief I felt at seeing a familiar face who knew the old me, not this supposed princess, made me rush up to him and fling my arms around his neck. Eli reciprocated my rather exuberant greeting, also grabbing hold of me and swinging me around, kissing me tenderly on the forehead. I giggled, breathing in his woody scent that immediately calmed the butterflies.

Just then I turned to see Isaac watching us with an angry look on his face. What was his problem? Glaring back at him I went to sit down at a table whilst Eli walked over to Isaac and started up what looked like an intense and heated conversation, however quiet they were trying to be. Every now and then I heard their raised voices and the words 'mutiny' and 'safety' being shared, which weren't exactly causing me to feel any better. Feeling twitchy I got up and moved, choosing to sit by the huge bay window instead and eat my apple.

Hearing the door close, I turned around to see Eli walking towards me once again, smiling. "Sorry about that," he said. "You've probably realised things are going to be tense in the meeting room this morning, and Isaac and I just wanted to go over the plan for your safety." He looked apologetic as he took my hand in his, rubbing his thumb over my palm soothingly. "We will be going in with you, as well as Janin and Taro, so you have nothing to worry about." He smiled reassuringly.

"Have you had a chance to see your family yet?" I asked curiously, wondering what he'd been doing since he left me last night.

"Actually yes, and they would love the honour of meeting you, especially Kayla." He grinned as I remembered that was his little sister.

As the dining room doors opened and I saw the Thills standing there expectantly, my stomach clenched realising the Council must be ready for me. I certainly didn't feel the same way. How was I ever supposed to be ready? I looked on as the four guardians took positions near me – all with determined expressions – and an ominous feeling settled in the pit of my stomach. I had no idea what I was going to say to Minen, let alone how to look at him. He had been responsible for the death of my parents and caused my whole life to change. I clenched my fists, my nails digging into my palms so hard I was drawing blood. Eli saw what I was doing and tried to soothe me by taking my hands in his and rubbing them gently.

Whilst waiting outside the Council chamber, I noticed the same emblem I had seen on Talawen's robe and asked Eli what it meant. "There are five symbols altogether, all intertwined with each other. The symbols represent the five elements and in the middle is a waterfall representing the 'Waterfall of Knowledge', which we passed on the way here. The waterfall is the entrance to the training ground where students who are to reach enlightenment are taught. It's kind of like human school. The waterfall symbolises the training Elves receive as a period of reflection and learning, which is of the utmost importance, hence it being part of our emblem. The students of today are key in helping to lead and protect our kingdom now and in the future." Good to know students my age were respected!

Without any further time for questions, the wooden doors leading into the chamber were opened and my first observations were of the large wooden table located in the middle of the room. Around the outer edge of one side of the table were six large ornate chairs, and seated on these were what I assumed to be the six Elders, judging by the green tunics they wore, just like Talawen's. On the other side sat an empty, solitary chair. Oh great, I thought sardonically, that must be for me.

Looking at the Elders' faces, I was relieved to see Talawen, who gave me an encouraging smile and a nod. Three of the other Elders smiled at me whilst two gave me looks of contempt. I didn't have to wait long to work out which one was Minen, as he stood up and plastered a greasy sneer on his face. His black hair was tied back and his beard made his face take on an even more sinister look. The hatred he clearly felt for me seemed to radiate through me in waves, yet his speech would have made you think I was his long lost daughter whom he loved dearly.

"Thea-Driel!" he exclaimed. "Thank goodness for your safe return! When you were taken all those years ago we felt sure you had been killed. Little did we know members of this very Council had taken it upon themselves to hide you away in the human world. Thank you, Talawen, for ensuring the safety of our most treasured, soon-to-be queen."

I could feel my blood beginning to boil as his fake smile seemed to stretch even further across his face. It took all my effort to remember Eli's words to stay calm. *Just breathe, you can do this,* I repeated to myself in a reassuring mantra.

Turning to look for Eli, I realised he was standing next to Isaac, just behind me, while Janin, Taro and the other four guards were strategically placed at various points around the room.

"Your concern for my safety is appreciated, Minen. I have been well looked after and am ready to embrace and honour my duty as queen," I said, facing him while addressing all of those seated. I was impressed that my voice hadn't shaken, considering how nervous I was.

"Let me formally introduce you to the other Council Elders," Minen continued, looking as though he was trying to torture me with his look of hatred. "To my right is Lhinanor, Elder to the Fire Elves," he started, as I looked upon the other face that had shown me such dislike when I first walked in. Good to know who my enemies were.

"Next we have Tanidor, Elder to the Water Elves…and on my left, Talawen, who you already are acquainted with. He is Elder to the Spirit Elves. Standing next to him is Elder Erwin of the Earth Elves, and finally Melwen here" – gesturing to a kindly looking man who appeared to be in his thirties, and definitely the youngest of the group – "is Elder to the Air Elves."

"It is a pleasure to meet you all," I started, hoping to sound in control. "And I look forward to getting to know each of you a lot better over the coming months, including understanding more about the different elements you wield as well as meeting those living in Aroben."

"I am sure Elves across the kingdom are already celebrating your safe return," Talawen enthused.

"Indeed, your arrival is all that has been talked about since last night," Minen began in a simpering voice.

"We, the Council Elders, are so glad you are ready to take to the throne as ruler of this great kingdom, and feel the Winter Solstice Ball would be an excellent setting for your coronation. It will also be an opportune moment for you to meet the other officials and notaries not only in Aroben, but also from the other kingdoms in Faery. That is…if you are in agreement, my princess," he finished, daring me to refuse.

"Of course," I replied.

Oh crap. I mean, I knew this moment was going to come, but hearing it out loud from the one man that wanted me dead was causing my brain to overload. Meeting lots of significant people was bad enough, let alone trying to look like I was capable of leading a kingdom. I'd been thrown into this world and I had no idea how to be a princess. How could Talawen and Eli, how could any of these people think I would be capable of this role? There was also a part of me that was surprised he seemed so willing to hand over the throne to me, but I didn't have to wait long to find out why.

Lost in my own thoughts, it took me a minute to realise everyone was staring at me, waiting for my answer, but to what I had no clue. "Your training? Are you ready to start?" Minen asked again, looking at me as though I were a complete imbecile.

"Yes of course," I said, waiting to see if I was going to be clued in a bit more as to what exactly they were talking about.

"Excellent! I look forward to receiving weekly updates, and Talawen," Minen said looking to his left, "seeing as you have been so…particular about Thea-Driel's safety, I will be making you personally responsible for ensuring she completes the training and reaches enlightenment just like any other Elf in training…before the ball, of course."

"Of course, it will be my honour," Talawen replied, inclining his head slightly.

Glancing behind me, the slight twitch to Isaac's jaw as he clenched his teeth, together with Eli's shocked face, made me realise something was seriously wrong. What had Minen said? I thought the meeting had gone pretty well.

"That went well," Eli said encouragingly as we walked back towards the courtyard, although his face painted a different picture.

"I don't believe you," I snapped at Eli, feeling my temper fraying as nerves seemed to set up a permanent camp in my stomach. Turning to Isaac in the hope of an honest answer I asked, "What did Minen say that was so wrong?"

Isaac just glared back at me with a stony expression; clearly he wasn't going to be any help. I looked back to Eli instead, waiting for his reply.

He sighed before speaking. "For you to be allowed to take up the throne, even though it's rightfully yours by birth, you need to complete the elemental training that Elves your age undertake, so that they can reach enlightenment. This would normally all be okay, but it can take an Elf a couple of years to complete this and fully harness the power of their element. You have until the Winter Ball – four months from now. I'm not quite sure how you're going to achieve that," he finished, rather unhelpfully.

"Hang on a minute, why the rush? Can't I just become queen some other time?"

"No Thea, you can't. Haven't you been listening to anything you've been told?" Isaac snapped. "Earthen Elves are being persecuted because of their element and now they're going missing. We don't have the luxury of time. And anyway, a coronation can only take place on the winter solstice to ensure whoever takes the throne will receive balance and harmony from the gods. Minen knows it's impossible. There's no way you can pass in that amount of time."

"What is your problem?!" I yelled back, not caring who heard. "You have no right to have a go at me! I can't make you out. Are you frustrated because you care or because I'm an inconvenience to you? One minute you seem normal and then..." I stopped, realising I was about to mention the heated looks I was sure he'd been giving me.

I glared at him, trying to ignore my body's insistence that I pounce on him and devour his lips. What was wrong with me? Growling, I stormed off, Eli following closely behind with a look of surprise on his face.

I couldn't cope with this, especially now that I had a

major problem on my hands, finally realising the predicament Minen had put me in and the near impossible task ahead of me.

SEVEN

TRAINING

It was a couple of days later and my mood hadn't exactly improved, especially towards Isaac, who fortunately seemed to be staying out of my way. The longer the better.

Dressed in training attire that consisted of black yoga pants, a short-sleeved black top and trainers, I pulled my hair back into a high ponytail and ran to the waterfall, knowing I was now ridiculously late. I had slept in, but to be fair I hadn't gotten to sleep until about three a.m. due to all the thoughts churning around in my head.

On arriving I saw Eli leaning against a rocky incline waiting for me as I ran up to him, panting from the sudden exertion.

"How can you be out of breath already?!" he exclaimed, raising his eyebrows.

Shrugging helplessly, I actually thought my breathlessness was more due to nerves.

We both turned toward the waterfall and 'oohed', impressed when we made it through to the other side without getting wet. There were definitely benefits of being in a world with magic. Glancing around, I gasped as I took in our new surroundings. We seemed to be in an enormous cave that had tunnels leading off into all different directions. Tiny crystals embedded into the rocks were glowing, giving the place a tranquil feel, and made me feel like we were looking up at the night sky.

Leading me down a path to the far right, Eli took me out onto a huge field that had groups of students of about my age dotted around, some stretching whilst others stood chatting. Blinking away the sudden brightness from being in the light again, I took a deep breath. Today was going to be very telling as to how I'd get on. The pressure I felt was immense.

"Err, where now?" I spluttered, trying to calm my breathing whilst hopping anxiously from one foot to another.

"Two of your classes, elemental training and Faey history, will be with the other students, but other than that you're going to be taught on a one-to-one basis."

"What? Why?" I groaned, thinking I didn't need to stand out as a lost cause with the other students any more than I already would.

"Well, the others have had at least a year's training already in hand-to-hand combat, whilst you haven't had any. There is no other way we can get you up to speed in time."

"Oh great," I huffed, as my stress levels kept rising.

"We don't even know what element you are affiliated with yet, although I think I can guess," he finished, looking at me like he had some big secret.

"What element is that then?" I enquired, curiosity winning through.

Eli smirked, knowing he had defused the ticking time bomb I was becoming.

"Fire," he stated authoritatively. "The protective shell you put around yourself the other day was orange and the heat that came off you was oppressive. Anyway, this element matches your personality!" he finished, snorting before doubling over in laughter.

"Har, har!" I growled back, giving him a withering look.

"What's yours?" I asked, realising I hadn't bothered to find out before now.

"I thought that would have been obvious from the Goblin fight. Air," he replied simply.

Of course, I thought, remembering how he had pushed the Goblin a considerable distance without even touching him.

"Let's get started then," I said impatiently, eager to see my fire abilities in action.

"Actually it's not me who will be training you. You have various instructors, and for weapon training and combat it's...." Eli trailed off apologetically as he pointed behind me.

Knowing luck had dealt me a blow, I turned to see none other than Isaac walking towards me, also dressed in black, the two daggers he kept either side of his hips now seeming even more intimidating. However, it wasn't the sight of the weapons that made my heart stop, it was the determined expression he wore. Oh gods, what did he have planned? It was then my trail of thought became distracted as I began to focus on how toned his muscles were, clearly visible under his t-shirt. Thoughts of wanting to do something a lot more personal than one-to-one combat training with him were creeping into my head. I could feel my face flush and turned around so my back was to him, and pretended to stretch just to give me back a few moments of sanity. My goodness, he was like Adonis and my insides were in turmoil as I tried to decide whether I wanted him to be my own personal trainer or not. On the one hand I would get to be in close contact with him and his yummy, delicious presence every day for the next four months. And his combat training gear – that certainly wasn't unpleasant to look at. On the other, he seemed so distant and formal and I didn't know how to act around him. Also, why did I still feel like I knew him? Not that I was going to ask him such a dorky question, especially as I was sure I was imagining the looks he was giving me.

When he was only a few yards away he gave me a nod. Eli took this as a cue to leave, but not before promising me that we would have lunch together later.

After giving a half wave to Eli, I turned back to Isaac and swallowed nervously, unsure of how he was going to behave, given our last meeting.

"Ok," he said, before his slow and steady gaze swept down my body. Blushing profusely again, I huffed before he finally looked back at my face. I was shocked to see a small smirk grace his lips.

Acting like nothing had happened, he then started to get down to business. Standing only a few steps from me, I was awash in his musky scent and felt immediately befuddled. If this was how delicious he smelt up close, there was no chance I was going to be able to concentrate.

"Firstly, you need to build up your core strength," he commanded. "I'm guessing you didn't keep up your fitness levels back in the human world?" he mocked, trying to provoke a reaction out of me.

Oh, it was going to be like that was it? I glared at him, knowing full well that I was toned due to all the running and other sports I did. Weighing in at about a hundred and ten pounds, I was certainly not overweight.

"Actually I was on the swim, hockey and ski teams at school," I retorted. Hah! I thought smugly, folding my arms ready for what he would say next.

His only response was to raise his eyebrows.

I'd show him.

Walking before me, he led me towards a nearby training room that had glass windows on two sides facing out onto the grounds. The interior was certainly impressive, as scattered around the room was everything you would need to set up your own gym. Even more impressive was the array of bows, daggers and swords of various lengths that hung on display across one of the walls, some in locked cabinets. The middle of the room was an open space covered with floor mats, on which we now stood.

"Welcome to your new home! Each morning we will do basic training in here and then you will go off to your other classes for the afternoon. Now, let's see how fit you really are," he challenged.

After nearly an hour of him making me do press-ups, circuit sprints and kickboxing, my sides were screaming in protest, but pride won through as I tried not to show how much of my energy was already spent and that I was completely exhausted. Hands on hips and bent over slightly whilst trying to stop a stitch that was becoming painful, I met his impassive expression with one full of determination.

"That was a good stretch, but when am I actually going to start learning something?" I taunted, trying to blow the hair that had become plastered on my forehead out of my eyes.

Looking bemused he shrugged, only answering, "Show me your fighting stance."

Ok, clearly I had no idea what to do. I mean, it wasn't like I had a brother I'd previously tried these moves out on, and with Eli, physical contact might have led to other things that had nothing to do with self-defence, I thought, grinning to myself.

Trying to remember the Kung Fu movies I'd seen, I stood with feet apart and arms raised to hip level. Whatever it was he had planned, I hoped he would go easy on me.

Why couldn't I have kept my mouth shut?! I sighed for the hundredth time as we again and again went through techniques that focused on my core balance. The main aim was to try to keep me at least standing when he came to attack, but on what must have been the thirtieth time of falling over, I could see the impatience beginning to show through on his face.

"Again," he sighed exasperatedly. "Four months Thea, that's all you've got. You have got to concentrate otherwise you won't be ready," he lectured, running his hand through his hair.

"I'm trying, okay?" I yelled back. "This is my first day, give me a break!"

"Fine, if this is the best you've got, let's call it a day. Tomorrow, six a.m. sharp, don't be late."

Oh great, my getting any sleep clearly wasn't on his agenda. He obviously hadn't seen how uncoordinated I was at that time of day. Feeling pissed and more than a little like I wanted to punch him, I left the gym and headed outside.

"That good?" Eli asked tentatively, looking at my bedraggled state. My hair was half out of my ponytail and I was limping due to a particularly bad fall. I just groaned and let him lead me off to lunch.

The afternoon was definitely something I was looking forward to as I'd be meeting the other students, and Eli had promised to keep me company. The purpose of my next class was to harness control of my element. It would also give me a chance to see how advanced others were with theirs.

Walking across the field we could make out someone waving frantically at us.

"Eli! Hey...Eli, I heard you were back!" a boy who seemed just a bit taller than me yelled. His dark brown hair was spiked, facing all different directions, and his three piercings, one in his eyebrow and two in his left ear, made me think he would definitely be fun to hang out with. He grinned with an infectious smile and his green eyes sparkled mischievously.

"Hi Baylin, long time no see! All is well I trust?" Eli called out, smiling back at him.

"Yup, I've been a model student of course." Baylin smirked, giving the impression he had been anything but.

"Of course." Eli grinned back. The girl standing next to Baylin gave me a timid smile and then bowed formally at me.

"You must be Thea-Driel...it is an honour to meet you," she said a little shyly. "I'm Inwen."

"Hi," I said, feeling shy back.

"And in case you didn't hear, I'm the one and only Baylin!" he said theatrically, bowing so low his hair swept the ground.

I laughed, feeling instantly relaxed around the two. Inwen's appearance was more like what I thought a traditional Elf would be, as she had blond hair that reached down to her waist and the same sparkling green eyes as Baylin. I wondered if they were related. She was my height and held herself gracefully, as though she were a dancer.

"It's good to meet you both. How long have you been training with your element for?"

"Eighteen months for me and fourteen for Inwen," Baylin jumped in.

"What element affinity do you both have?" I asked curiously.

Inwen answered this time. "Air, and Bay's is earth."

Just then the professor called everyone to attention and put us all into groups. Fortunately I was partnered with Eli, who explained that he would guide me through the basics the others had already covered.

The purpose of the lesson was to call your element to you and be able to manipulate it around a nearby object. As mine was a piece of wood, the aim was obviously to see if I could set it on fire.

After an hour of squinting furiously at the pathetic flame I had created in front of me, all I had managed to do was make it travel to where the piece of wood sat about a metre away, but then nothing else would happen. Whilst I was frustrated by my lack of fire, Eli seemed rather impressed. Looking around I realised most of the other students had created the desired effect, but Eli reassured me it was only because they had had longer to practice. I tried to take comfort in this as I thought over how much I had to accomplish in such a little time.

What with the morning's physical training, the afternoon seemed to have zapped me emotionally and I was so ready for some downtime. Making my way back to the others, Eli caught up the instructor with my progress.

"So Thea-Driel, are you allowed to have fun before you become queen?" Baylin teased.

"Baylin!" Inwen exclaimed, smacking him on the arm. "You can't talk to the princess like that, Thea-Driel is going to be our queen!" she hissed, glaring at him.

"Please, call me Thea. I just want to be treated normally. And after the day I've had, the answer is most definitely YES! Although I'm not quite sure what you do for fun around here. What did you have in mind?"

"There's a party being held by a group of Water Elves Saturday night. It would be great if you could come!" Baylin pleaded. "I know Inwen would like a girl to hang out with instead of her big brother!"

"Brother!" I exclaimed. "I thought you both had the same eyes, but everything else about you both is so different!"

"Hey, enough with the 'big'," Inwen replied, whacking him in the stomach. Turning to me she continued. "Bay is one minute older than me, he's my twin, and because he started his training a few months before me, he thinks he's the big chief around here!" She laughed, showing obvious love and affection for him.

"I'd love to come," I said excitedly. "Just let me

sound Eli out first and I'll get back to you." I was feeling really thankful they had included me. Hopefully I'd just made some new friends.

As I observed the other students milling around, my eyes fell to those of a boy standing around a group who didn't look as friendly as the others. They somehow looked meatier than the other Elves and were hunched over whispering, like they were up to no good. The weird thing was the boy I was now having a staring contest with seemed completely out of place. He even stood slightly apart from them, like he didn't want to be there.

"Who's that?" I asked, gesturing to the boy as he finally turned away from me.

Judging by the looks of disgust on both the twins' faces, I guessed he wasn't a friend of theirs.

"That's Callon and his group of idiot followers. They're all Fire Elves and so think they're all that, especially with Callon's dad being Council Elder Lhinanor."

Oh great, another member of the 'I hate Thea' club, I thought, as I remembered how his dad had glowered at me like Minen had, obviously preferring me dead rather than alive. Scrutinising him further, whilst I could see the family resemblance in build and colour of hair and eyes, Callon's facial expression was the complete opposite of his father's. When he was staring at me, his expression held sympathy and something else I couldn't quite place.

"Stay away from them, they're bad news," Baylin continued, snapping me out of my reverie.

"Thanks again for the invite," I said, realising Eli was coming back. "I guess I'll see you tomorrow...it was good to meet you," I said, smiling at Inwen as I watched them walking off in a different direction to the one we were heading in.

"So...fancy going somewhere quiet?" Eli asked as we walked over to the lake by the palace. I nodded gratefully, glad he knew me so well and that I really needed to be with just him.

We sat in companionable silence for a good couple of hours, watching as twilight came and with it hundreds of stars that filled the sky. My mind filtered through everything I had done that day.

Eli began to hum a tune I wasn't familiar with, and turned on his side to face me while he stroked my hair, occasionally brushing his thumb across my cheek, making it tingle. I too turned over so I could snuggle into him, and rested my head in the crook of his neck.

After a while he moved to look into my eyes and I saw the intense look of passion that burned there. I cringed inwardly. Since my feelings for Isaac were becoming stronger and stronger, maybe I really did just see Eli like a brother, who I loved greatly, but no more than that. After he had spent my whole life guarding me, I had no idea how I was going to tell him this. It would break his heart, especially if he knew who held my affections, whether they were unrequited or not. I still felt Isaac was hiding something.

Groaning to myself, I feigned sleepiness and snuggled up close to him once again, waiting for a revelation to hit and tell me what I was supposed to do.

EIGHT

NORMALITY...IF THERE IS SUCH A THING?

I began to get into a routine over the next couple of days, which mainly consisted of training, training and more training. There were only two days until the party but I still hadn't asked if I could go. Part of me wanted to be honest, but I had this sneaky suspicion that Eli - who would in turn ask Isaac - would say no because of my safety. Or they would say yes and come along with me. I doubted me crashing the party with a whole bunch of Thill guards would go down well. This therefore meant the only solution I could think of was to say nothing at all and just sneak out and go. Luckily Inwen and Baylin understood my predicament and were more than happy to help me plan my escape, promising not to say anything.

The next couple of days dragged on. I was

desperate to have some fun, and although I could tell I was already becoming a lot fitter, Isaac was still incredibly hard on me.

"Again," he sighed in frustration.

We were still working on developing my defensive techniques, which consisted of me being able to duck and weave around my opponent without being hit or knocked over first. The last attempt was definitely going to leave another bruise. Not that I would have said anything to Isaac, but I was really suffering physically and was sure this was due to the intensive regime my body suddenly had to endure. My inability to out-manoeuvre my opponent also wasn't helped by the fact that over half of my body was covered in bruises, making me stiff and sore.

"Thea, you must concentrate," he urged. "Minen's men, especially the Goblin associates he chooses to spend time with, will be a lot tougher on you than I've been, and they will use their elemental magic on you as well."

Swallowing down tears of frustration and hurt I turned to face him again, wiping sweat from my forehead onto my sleeve. Couldn't he see I was trying my hardest? I didn't need to be told again what pressure I was under.

Just then, to my relief, I saw Eli coming through the door, which could only mean this torture session was about to end and he was there to take me to lunch.

Focusing back on Isaac, I took a deep breath and moved just in time to the left, ducking under his arm as he thrust out towards me. Managing to miss that, he then twisted to the right and kicked out his leg towards me, expecting me to move. This is what I would have normally done, but I was so exhausted all I could do was freeze. As if in slow motion, I watched as his leg made contact with my knee, and hearing the snap that ensued, I knew something was seriously wrong.

I screamed in anguish as I fell to the floor in pain, jarring my back in the process.

"Thea! Are you okay?" Isaac exclaimed worriedly as he knelt beside me, trying to touch my knee to look at the damage without making it worse.

"All my gods, Thea," Eli shouted as he ran into the room after seeing what had happened and knelt down on my other side. I turned my body towards him, trying to seek comfort as a steady stream of tears ran down my face. There was no way I could pretend everything was fine and all I could do was croak out a whimper.

"Thea, what were you thinking? That was a basic move. What's wrong with you?" Isaac snapped, swallowing down the glimmer of kindness I had just witnessed.

Turning back to face him I could feel my anger bubbling over again, no matter how much pain I was in. Who did he think he was?

"What's wrong with me?" I hissed, trying to breathe through the agony I was in. "I've done everything you've asked, and I'm sorry if it's not good enough for you."

I then let out a groan as a slight movement to my knee sent pains shooting up my body.

"Look, I'm sorry...I just need—" He tried to continue before Eli interrupted him.

"Stop! That's enough." Eli glared at us both, shocking me that he would speak to his superior like that even though he was a friend. "Thea, how are you holding up? You're not looking too great," he said anxiously. Trust Eli to state the obvious.

I leaned back so my head was resting on the mat and closed my eyes. Feeling faint and like I could throw up at any moment, I tried to breathe deeply as tears continued to leak down my face. I could feel one of them pulling up my pant leg to assess the damage.

Hearing a hiss from Eli, I braved a look and saw my knee had already swollen up to twice its original size, and my kneecap was completely off-centre. Seeing this caused a second wave of nausea to hit and I clamped my mouth shut, refusing to vomit in front of them.

"Thea," Isaac said gently. "We're going to need to take you to a healer, and to do that we're going to have to move you."

Letting out another groan, I opened my eyes to see the worried expressions passing between the two of them. "How bad is it?" I whispered, trying to keep my voice steady.

"Your kneecap is dislocated," Eli said sympathetically.

The tears wouldn't stop. It wasn't just this ridiculous situation I had gotten into with Isaac that was making me upset, but everything else that had happened to me in the last year came tumbling back. From my parents' death, to finding out that they weren't actually my biological parents, and then to leaving behind the life I knew and having to take on the responsibilities of leading a kingdom in a world I never knew existed. The situation I was in came crashing down around me.

Eli scooped me up carefully, using Isaac to support my knee with the gentlest of pressure. I snuggled into him, trying to hide my face as embarrassment at my emotional outburst set in. I might have been in a terrible emotional state and in a lot of pain, but I still remembered that these were two of the hottest guys I knew.

I didn't pay much attention to Eli and Isaac's conversation as they took me to get help, preferring instead to just keep my eyes closed and zone out. I focused on breathing in and out slowly through the pain that was made worse with even the slightest of movements, however hard they tried not to jolt me.

After a couple of minutes, I knew we had arrived at the medical centre due to the pungent smell of antiseptic wafting up my nose. Opening my eyes, I saw I was being placed on a medical bed in a bright, airy room, and seconds later an Elf in a white coat – who I presumed was a healer – walked over to me.

"Thea-Driel, it is an honour to meet you, although I wish it could be under better circumstances," he said, smiling down kindly at me. "I'm Healer Farwen. Tell me what happened."

Isaac decided to jump in at this point. "We were practising basic defence techniques when Thea got kicked in the knee. It looks dislocated," he stated anxiously, searching my face to see if I was feeling any better.

After a painful examination, the healer confirmed it was dislocated and put his hands over my knee, closing his eyes in concentration. It was then I began to feel warmth spreading through the damaged area and the pain began to lessen. When he had finished, Farwen taped it up with a bandage and gave me some funny-tasting liquid for pain relief.

Seeing my look of surprise at what he had done, Farwen began to speak.

"Now," he started. "I'm aware you are currently

being taught about Elf history, but you may not yet know that healers are able to wield spirit, which means I can speed up the healing process. That and the fact that Elves heal quicker than humans means you should be as good as new in a week," Farwen announced.

"That's great," I said feeling much better at the thought that I would still have a chance to pass the enlightenment test before the Winter Solstice Ball. Eli and Isaac also visibly relaxed.

"Use these crutches to assist you with walking for as long as you need them." He smiled again. "And good luck with your training. You are a light to us in dark times and I look forward to the changes your return will bring," he finished, squeezing my hand.

Even with the pain medication, a headache had begun to make an appearance and it throbbed when I tried to sit up. I rubbed my forehead tiredly and grimaced at the pain I was still in, desperate to wallow in self-pity back in my own bed.

"Come on then, time for you to rest back at the palace," Eli said softly as he scooped me up, once again coming to my rescue.

"Hey! I can walk," I protested feebly, painfully aware I must have looked dreadful and was desperately in need of a shower after this morning's workout.

"Your Highness, I'm your guardian and I'm going to look after you," he commanded with a hint of possessiveness. He gave me one of his sexy smiles. Grinning, I turned to look at Isaac, who still wore a pained expression on his face.

"I'm fine, I promise," I whispered, as he turned to give me a fixed smile. He and I needed to talk. I was sure I wasn't the only one who felt the tension between us.

NINE

A LESSON IN DRINKING TOO MUCH

The day of the party had arrived and my knee was making a fairly quick recovery as predicted, which was a relief. Since the accident Eli and Isaac had spent most of the time fussing over me, which hadn't allowed me much time to relax. Luckily, with the party on our doorstep, the twins and I had come up with a plan to get me there without either of my guards knowing. Time away from them was just what I needed.

We told them Inwen and I had decided to have a girls' day and that I would be staying overnight at her house. This worked out great since it meant Inwen and I could get to know each other better, as well as get ready for the party together. I also now had an alibi for being out all night!

Isaac and Eli agreed with the plans for me to stay at Inwen's on the condition that Janin and Taro were to be stationed outside the front of her parents' home. Not a problem, when we would be sneaking out the back!

"I didn't think they were ever going to leave!" Inwen giggled as she shut the door after Isaac and Eli had left, satisfied that the other guards were in position.

"Tell me about it!" I exclaimed as I hobbled up the stairs to her room. "Since the knee incident they've been hovering around me non-stop!" I joked. "Actually, poor Isaac seems to have taken it to heart and every time he looks at me I can see the guilt he feels. He's been completely unbearable since I first met him, but I know he cares about me and is very protective of my safety." I smiled coyly.

"Ooh, you like him, don't you?!" Inwen yelled, throwing a pillow at me.

"What's not to like?" I smirked back, relieved to finally tell someone how I was feeling.

"I thought Eli had stolen your heart? The way he looks at you…" Inwen continued.

I groaned before trying to explain. "Well, this is part of the problem; I do love Eli but we've never had 'the talk'. You know, the one where you decide if it's worth risking your friendship to find out if there is something more? Eli and Isaac are so different, yet perfect at the same time. With Eli everything feels safe. He's known me such a long time, knows all my quirky habits and would do anything for me. Isaac is the unknown. He's the strong, silent and mysterious type. He drives me crazy but at the same time the thought of being far away from him is painful. Isaac's like a drug I'm completely addicted to. Help!" I wailed at her, feeling conflicted.

"Ahh, the classic torn-between-two-men conundrum, I don't envy you," she grinned. "However, I do have my own issues. Being Baylin's sister has put me in the 'strictly off-limits' category with all of his friends and any other male student who dares to look my way!" Inwen snorted in frustration. "There is someone I like though. He's called Logan and I think he kind of likes me too, and he'll be there tonight!" she squealed happily.

"Okay, well we are going to have to get you all dressed to impress. What do you wear to a party around here?" I asked.

Just before it was time to leave, we stood looking in the mirror, suitably pleased with our efforts. Luckily, fashion trends in Aroben weren't that different to those in the human world. Inwen looked great in a short black dress with a green pendant that hung on a silver chain, matching the colour of her eyes. I had borrowed a light blue dress that stopped just above my knees, and wore the bracelet my parents back in the human world had given me. It was silver metal with a charm that Inwen explained had the Elven symbols for strength and courage on it. I smiled to myself, realising in that moment they must have given it to me as they knew the struggles I would face, as a daily reminder to remind me of their love and that they were still with me.

She had styled our hair, with mine in a loosely tied side chignon, with a few wisps pulled out so they fell naturally around my face, and she had opted for an elegant French twist.

"Ladies," Baylin said, entering Inwen's room. "Looking lovely as always, ready for the great escape?!"

With determined nods we talked through the plan to sneak out. Baylin and Inwen's parents had no idea that the Thills didn't know what we had planned, or that I hadn't told them, therefore the guards would still be stationed outside their home, none the wiser.

Walking down the stairs, I sneaked out into the back garden and waited for Bay and Inwen to say goodbye to their parents, and after getting a couple of hundred yards from their house, I released I had been holding my breath.

"Phew…we've made it!" I exclaimed and chanced a look behind me, grinning as there was no sign of either of my guards.

After a short while, we heard the party before seeing it. The music had been cranked up really loud and the sub-woofer was causing my whole body to vibrate. Turning down a path, we came to a cluster of houses near a river and could see the party was in full swing with at least thirty people milling around outside.

Upon arrival, we were greeted by a group of students I recognised from training, and as soon as they saw Baylin there was a loud cheer to which Inwen just grinned, rolling her eyes at his reception. He was immediately swallowed up as he entered the house, heading in the direction of the dance floor. Inwen and I made a more discreet entrance, choosing to first get a drink.

Peering at the makeshift bar, I looked on curiously at the blue liquid sitting in two huge bowls. "You'll love this," Inwen shouted at me over the music, holding up two overflowing cups for us. "They contain juice from the Faila fruit. It's really sweet and tastes delicious. This drink is famous at parties, but if you've never had any, it can get you drunk fast..."

Grabbing the drink I took a sip, enjoying the tropical taste. We moved onto the dance floor, standing near the edge so I felt more at ease that my knee wasn't going to get bumped into. Looking around I realised we were getting lots of looks, and turned to Inwen to see if she had noticed.

"It's because of who you are," she said, amused. "As well as because of how gorgeous you look! You certainly are the belle of the ball!" She giggled.

"Hardly!" I retorted, feeling embarrassed by the attention. "Give me that," I demanded, taking Inwen's drink and downing it in one. "Much better!" I said, giggling along with her, already feeling more relaxed and less self-conscious.

As the music changed to something more upbeat, Baylin came over to us with another round of drinks and a couple of friends in tow.

"Are you having fun?" he grinned at me, handing me another drink. "These are my friends Tharlin and Logan," he continued. "They wanted to come and get acquainted," he smirked, waggling his eyebrows at me.

Seeing the look Logan gave Inwen, I realised this was the Elf she liked and was bemused that Baylin had no idea there was something going on between his friend and his sister. The looks they were giving each other were making it really obvious.

"What happened?" Tharlin inquired, looking down at my bandaged knee.

"Training," I groaned sheepishly. Remembering the humiliation at the time, I gulped down more of my drink.

As Baylin, Tharlin and I chatted, I realised Inwen and Logan had sneaked off. It didn't bother me that she had left. I knew Bay would look after me, and judging by the looks Tharlin kept giving me, I realised he wasn't going to be going anywhere soon either.

The party was in full flow now, with those on the dance floor packed together like cattle, and the heat and drink meant I was beginning to feel really light-headed and needed to get some fresh air. Luckily at that moment Inwen came back to join us and explained to Baylin where we were heading.

The party was still very much in swing outside as well, but at least the fresh air meant I managed to wake up a bit.

"Oh my gods, Logan is so hot!" Inwen squealed, jumping up and down. "He said he has liked me for ages but was keeping his distance because of Bay!"

"That's great Inwen!" I enthused back, happy for my friend.

"Now we just have to sort out your man trouble. Let me get us a drink to help with that!" She laughed, running back inside.

Feeling relaxed and content for the first time in ages, I looked around to see who else was out here. Immediately, my eyes were drawn to a bunch of rowdy guys who were loudly shouting rude comments to some partygoers nearby. Tuning in on what they were saying, I realised they were having a go at some guys because of their earth affinity.

Inwen came back at that moment and handed me some more Faila juice, which I downed again, distracted by what was going on.

"Whoa, steady Thea! I think you've had enough," she commented as I stumbled slightly.

Just then the fight got physical, and drew in a big crowd, many coming from inside the house, including Baylin and co. Turning back towards the scuffle, I saw Callon standing with the rowdy guys and realised they were the ones he had been hanging around with the other day. Surprisingly though, instead of a look of delight on his face at what his friends were doing, he watched on with a look of disgust, as though he would rather be anywhere else but there.

That was when things took a turn for the worse. I wanted to blame it on the drink, but there was another part of me that was getting pissed with the idea that some punked-up Elves thought they were better than everyone else due to the element they could wield. I knew this was a belief they had grown up with and thought their actions were normal because of Minen, but I couldn't stop the anger building when I remembered my parents who had fought hard against this ideology and had been murdered for it.

Storming over, I was just about to give my opinion and try push the boys apart – not one of my brightest ideas, since they were at least a foot taller than I was, and I also had a damaged knee – when Callon grabbed hold of me, trying to pull me back. My drunken state and defunct limb meant I toppled back into him.

"Don't get involved, it's none of your business," he snapped as I tried to right myself.

"It is my business," I retorted. "When I take over as

queen I'm going to put an end to this nonsense. You are no better than anyone else. In fact, you're worse, because you're choosing to accept things the way they are and not fighting against it. Can't you see it's wrong?!"

The twins, including Logan and Tharlin, came over to back me up in case I needed it. However, I was on a roll, so I ignored them and continued to focus my attention on Callon.

"I know who your father is. Don't think I don't know what he stands for, and you're one of them," I yelled.

"I have no choice," he growled. "I won't ever get a choice," he muttered to himself as he walked away.

Surprised by his response, I was thrown for a minute and just stared after him, totally oblivious to what was going on next to me. It was only on hearing Baylin shouting my name in alarm that I turned in time to see a small white disc come flying towards me. It hit me in the forehead. Everything then went blank.

"Tell me again what happened," a familiar voice growled as Inwen sobbed, replaying the events of the night before, when I had been knocked out.

Blinking and trying to take in my surroundings, I realised how cold I was and that I was lying on the ground outside in the garden. Bay and Inwen were trying their hardest to answer Isaac's questions without getting us all, and in particular me, in a whole heap of trouble.

"Thea!" Isaac exclaimed, relieved to see I was awake. "Don't move. You have a nasty cut on your head and I need to stop the bleeding."

I winced as he touched my head, thinking there was no way I was going to move, especially as everything was spinning unpleasantly. Inwen looked down at me with frightened eyes and I tried to reassure her, with a half-smile half-grimace, that I was fine, but I don't think it worked.

After a couple of minutes, Isaac had finished whatever he was doing and looked down at me, concern written all over his face.

"I don't know what on earth you were doing at this party, Thea-Driel, so help me! You should be taking your safety seriously. Whether it's at a simple party or the threat of Goblins coming after you, it makes no difference. You are too important to the future of Aroben to be so foolish."

The obvious disappointment and the quiet manner in which he spoke made me feel even worse.

"And you," he said, turning back to Bay and Inwen, "should have known better. You have a better understanding of what life has been like here, especially with all the training you have received, yet all you have done is allow her to be placed in more danger."

Both siblings looked down guiltily. Wishing a hole would swallow me up, Isaac looked back at me.

"I've done the best I can, but I'm going to need to get you to a healer. Can you walk?" he asked frowning.

"Yes, no problem," I said, not wanting to be any further bother than I already was. However, once I stood, everything tipped sideways. Isaac grabbed hold of me, making sure I didn't fall flat on the floor again.

"What were you drinking?" he asked me suspiciously, whilst still trying to keep me upright. I knew he could tell my wobbliness was more than a result of my bump.

"She only had a couple...she had never tried...I

only gave…" Inwen tried to explain. "It was Faila juice," she finished sheepishly.

Isaac's jaw tensed as he fought to hold back whatever he wanted to say. Then, ignoring me completely, he turned to Janin and Taro, who I hadn't realised had been standing next to me the entire time.

Oh crap. Another round of guilt washed over me as I realised I had gotten them into trouble too as they obviously hadn't known where I was.

"I'm going to carry her back. Make sure they get back safely," he said in exasperation, nodding towards the twins.

Giving them a defeated look, I braced myself as Isaac scooped me up gently, careful to avoid my knee that, along with everything else, had started throbbing again. Unable to stop what my body wanted, I leaned into his warm embrace, breathing in his intoxicating fragrance. His smell reminded me so much of home and security. Letting out a deep sigh, I gingerly felt my forehead, wincing again as another round of throbbing began to drum away in my head.

"You are lucky the hodan you got hit with was only made of plastic, otherwise you would have been more seriously injured."

I stayed quiet, not sure how I was going to start apologising for all the idiotic things I realised I had done.

"Hey…Thea?" he asked, worried by my silence. "Are you okay? Do you need me to stop? We're almost there," he tried to ask calmly, concerned by my quietness. He unconsciously pulled me closer.

"No…I mean yes…I'm fine. Isaac, I'm so sorry I was such an idiot…I didn't think…I just wanted to do something normal. It was stupid of me," I mumbled.

"Don't say any more for now, let's just check that you're okay," he said in a soft tone as we arrived at the healer centre.

Two hours later and back at the palace, I collapsed on my bed, my last thoughts about the trouble I was going to be in tomorrow and groaning at the thought of how unpleasant that would be.

TEN

YOU REAP WHAT YOU SOW

"I can't believe you were so stupid!" Eli scolded as he walked into Talawen's office. "There are some real idiots out there and getting involved in their fight was the last thing you should have done." He looked at me like he wanted to shake and hug me all at the same time. "You know we would have let you go with security…"

"I'm sorry, I've already said that I realised it was a stupid thing to do," I said remorsefully, whilst looking back at Talawen and Isaac, hoping they would support my statement.

"Thea realises her mistake Eli. However, it has highlighted that perhaps…err…her security detail needs to be revised," Talawen suggested tentatively, looking at Isaac.

I groaned at my stupidity and the realisation hit that I would now be even more closely followed, especially by my two strictest guards.

"We have already made the arrangements, Talawen, and again, my apologies for not performing our duty. We had thought Thea would be more willing to help us keep her safe, but apparently not, therefore we have taken this into our own hands," Isaac started stiffly.

"Of course, Minen heard about the events at the party from Lhinanor and his nephew. Whilst he passed on his best for a speedy recovery from your head injury, I would imagine he was secretly pleased this unfortunate incident has happened so early on. I wouldn't put it past him to try and tarnish your reputation before you have even become queen. He will want you to appear young and irresponsible, and I'm sorry to say but you've just played into his hands."

I nodded, acknowledging again to myself what an idiot I had been. If the situation wasn't so serious it would have been comical as Eli and Isaac both towered over me, arms folded with fierce expressions on their faces. I was going to have to make it up to them big time – that is, if I were ever allowed out again.

The next half an hour consisted of hearing who would be following me when and where. Basically either Isaac or Eli would be with me at all times, along with three other Thills. Three!

Talawen listened on sympathetically, knowing how difficult this would be for me but also knowing that I had brought this on myself.

Walking back to one of the reception rooms, I reflected on the fact that, including the knee incident, I had wasted well over a week of training, which left me just under three months of training left. I had to sort myself out.

Almost as though Isaac could read my thoughts he stated, "Now that your knee is pretty much healed, we need to get back to training, starting now," indicating that I should follow him to the training grounds. I said goodbye to Eli, who had agreed we would meet up as usual for lunch, and headed after Isaac and the other three guards. Looking at their unfamiliar faces, they didn't acknowledge me, which made me think Isaac must have filled them in on what I had done, and I walked dejectedly, hoping that I would see a friendly face or even the twins later.

As I blocked, turned and twisted, managing to stay on my feet each time, I took a furtive glance at Isaac to see his reaction. Seeing the corners of his mouth quirk up every now and then into a ghost of a smile, I knew he was impressed.

"Good, Thea, I'm pleased you are beginning to take this seriously. Your foot work is a lot better and you're even beginning to pre-empt some of my moves. Well done!"

Feeling proud of my achievements, Isaac and I went to find Eli, where I was officially handed over, and after a quick lunch we headed to Elemental History, which had so far been a little dry in content. Don't get me wrong, it was completely fascinating to learn about a kingdom and Faery realm that I had never heard of, especially because of my royal line, but so far my brain had been filled with date after date from so long ago, I was finding it difficult to see the relevance. However, today would be different.

Our professor was an Elf called Pellam, who had long, dark brown hair that he tied back into a ponytail.

Even though he looked about thirty, his conversations about events he had witnessed hundreds of years ago obviously meant he was much older than he appeared.

"Where do you think our magic comes from?" he started, staring around at the students sitting in a loose semi-circle outside. I'm guessing Elves didn't feel the need to be in classrooms like back in the human realm.

"That's easy," a girl replied, I think her name was Salean. "We draw the magic from our surroundings. The energy in the air provides us with what we need and if we are closer to the element we have an affinity with, our magic becomes stronger."

"That's right, and why do we have an affinity with only one element, why not all five?" he said provocatively.

"So that we know who is strong and who is weak," one of the goons from the party piped up. Fortunately, Salean hit him for me as I realised Eli was pleading with me to ignore what he had just said and not start another fight.

"Your foolish answer is why we have so many problems in our society, Rhonir," Pellam scolded. Rhonir just looked back at him defiantly.

"Contrary to what some Elves say," he continued, "the goddess Elebrin gave us each unique gifts, to be able to use an element – and only one – so that all Elves would be united in their goal to achieve harmony, love and respect across the whole kingdom. Her thinking was that everyone would need to work together to use their gift for the greater good. No one Elf would be able to do this on their own. This was the way of our kingdom for thousands of years, until recently, when Minen felt Elves should be put into a hierarchical system. Now we live in a world where Fire Elves are seen by some as the most valued," he explained, as Rhonir and a few others cheered.

"Recognising each Elf's value in society is something we must all embrace," Pellam continued carefully, not wanting to say anything against Minen that would get him into trouble. "All elementals are integral to our survival. Earth Elves," he continued, identifying those viewed as the most inferior, "have great command of the land around us. We must not belittle how powerful they really are."

"I've heard Earth Elves are beginning to disappear," said a boy called Bronid. "My dad's friend, who is an Earth Elf, can't be found anywhere, and my sister's friend who also wields earth has gone missing too."

"Yeah, I've heard about Elves going missing too," Salean piped up. "Where are they going?"

An uncomfortable feeling came over the group as even Rhonir seemed perturbed by what the others were saying.

"You're right," Pellam answered hesitantly. "There has been talk of some Elves going missing and this is being looked into. In the meantime, remember how we are each important in this great kingdom of ours," he finished, clearly feeling the need to end this conversation.

As Eli and I got up to walk to my next class, my mind was reeling from what I had just heard. Thinking Eli would know more, I brought up the subject with him.

"There have been murmurings of something going on that has caused many to feel unsettled, but to be honest, I don't know too much because guarding you has been a full time job." He chuckled softly.

Not feeling satisfied with his answer, I knew at

some point I had to find out more, I just wasn't sure how.

The last class of the day was elemental training, which I was most looking forward to as I would finally see the twins. Seeing them in the distance, I waved and hobbled quickly across, hoping for a few moments alone with them before my entourage caught up.

"Did you get in lots of trouble?" Inwen asked sympathetically. "How's your head?" she continued in the same breath. Then without waiting for an answer, she gave me a big squeeze.

"Well, other than now having to put up with four guardians following me around and Isaac and Eli not trusting me at all, it's okay." I sighed. "I'm sorry if you got in trouble as well. Were your parents mad?" I said to Bay.

"Nah, we've come through unharmed!" he joked. "I guess you'll have to lay off the parties for a while, huh?"

"Yes, but with the Winter Ball coming up soon, I could really do with your help with extra training as well as with something I just found out," I said, filling them in on the Elf disappearances. Seeing their shocked faces, I realised this was news to them as well. Fortunately, one of their cousins worked for the Council and they promised they would see what they could find out. Eli chose that moment to come over and join us, giving Bay and Inwen frowns, reminding them he wasn't impressed with their latest party exploits, but they didn't say any more.

Callon was also in our elemental lesson, but I chose to ignore him, still not quite sure what his problem was. Whatever it was, he didn't want his father or friends knowing about it. At the end of the session I felt really happy with my success as I seemed to have a much better hold of my ability to control fire. This lesson focused on our ability to manipulate our elements from different distances – and for me and the other Fire Elves, to manipulate fire to help us carry out different tasks.

I smirked at Eli and turned to see how everyone else was getting on. It was then that I noticed Inwen struggling over her hold of a mini tornado she was trying to move. Realising her tornado was getting dangerously close to where the Fire Elves had been practising, I called out to Eli as I ran to help. The professor had also realised what was happening and cried out to me and others to move out of the way.

"I can't stop it! There's too much energy...I can't hold on!" she screamed.

"Help her!" Bay panicked as he caught up with me and looked on in fear for his sister.

Instinct took over and, before anyone else could react, I held out my palms facing forward and willed myself to take a hold of the tornado Inwen was controlling, kind of like how I did when controlling fire. Slowly I began to feel its energy become a part of my being and gasped at how different it felt to wielding fire. This magic was beautiful and, although very deadly, I could feel that it had a life of its own, like it was its own entity.

Going into a trance, I concentrated harder, now focusing solely on trying to move the tornado away from the fire, and directed it instead into the forest behind. Using more and more energy from within me, the tornado eventually began to move out of harm's way, becoming less and less ferocious, until thankfully it became a gentle breeze before disappearing altogether.

Knowing that at last everyone was safe, I sucked in a breath and turned to look at Inwen just as black spots began to cloud my vision. Realising just then how exhausted I was, my trembling legs refused to hold my weight any longer and I collapsed to the ground, hearing Eli calling my name as I succumbed to the darkness.

ELEVEN

WELL, WHO WOULD HAVE GUESSED?!

Coming to, I slowly peered up into Healer Farwen's face to see him smiling back down at me, his eyes sparkling in delight.

"Been getting up to mischief again have you, Thea?" he chuckled, as I turned to see that Eli and Isaac were in the room as well. They, however, obviously thought this situation was anything but funny as both were frowning down at me. What a surprise. Eli then leaned over and began rubbing circles soothingly on my hand, like he needed the contact to make sure I was alright.

"What happened?" I asked hazily, waiting for my memories to catch up with me.

"You proved again how extraordinary you are," Isaac said softly.

"Oh!" I answered as I suddenly remembered.

"How did you do it?" Eli asked. "It's very, very rare to be able to control two elements, but I suppose if anyone was going to do it, you would!" he said with affection.

At that moment there was a soft knocking at the door and Talawen peered around the corner. "Ahh, you're awake," he said, relieved. "Baylin and Inwen will be pleased to know that, they are waiting outside most anxiously."

"What happened?" I directed my question at Talawen, shocked by what I had been able to achieve.

"What indeed?" he replied. "My only guess is that there is more to you than we first thought. It is a great honour to be chosen by the goddess to wield two elements. I wonder…" he said, pausing to look around. "Have you actually tried to control any other elements?"

"No," I replied. "Eli saw me controlling fire when we were attacked by Goblins, so we assumed that was what I had an affinity with. We never thought to see if I could influence anything else."

"It's interesting how you are able to manipulate your magic to greater effect if your friend's lives are in danger. Your ability to wield the elements definitely seems linked to your emotions, allowing the magic to become stronger and more powerful. If you think back, that's probably how you were able to fight the Goblins, because you feared for your own and Eli's lives."

Isaac and Eli looked at each other with smug expressions.

"What now?!" I sighed at them, beginning to feel completely out of the loop with what was going on.

"Well, princess," Isaac spoke, "knowing you now

have a secret weapon that others, including Minen, don't know about, can only help to keep you safer," he said, clearly pleased by this unexpected outcome.

"But what about those who saw what I did? By morning everyone will know what happened and my secret will be out."

"Actually, you intervened so quickly the only ones who realised your involvement were the professor, the other Thill guards and the twins – all of whom have been sworn to secrecy," Eli announced.

"Minen not knowing is definitely to our advantage," Talawen confirmed. "With Professor Gonan's help, as training Elves to use their element is his speciality, I would like you to explore what else you can do with your magic. The sooner the better," he finished.

"I can't," I said again, frustrated.

Professor Gonan was trying to get me to harness spirit magic and use it to manipulate the emotions he was feeling, while Isaac, Bay and Inwen watched on in support. We'd had great success in getting me to wield water, much to my amusement, as whichever guards I had protecting me would end up very wet by the end of the session. I had also managed to use earth magic in different ways that included making plants grow at an alarming rate and creating landslides. The last element – spirit – was the one I was definitely having the most difficulty with. Every time I tried to take hold of its magic, it made me feel strange, almost intoxicated, and therefore trying to keep a clear head whilst changing a person's emotions was proving extremely difficult. Apparently, because Spirit Elves were the rarest types of Elf, they were therefore the least understood, but at least Gonan was able to give me some direction in what to do, especially being a spirit user himself.

"What I can share," the professor started by saying, "is that controlling an Elf's emotions has to be undertaken with the most honest of intentions, because you have an unfair advantage over others. Think for example of the amount of power and influence you could have at Council meetings or when dealing with affairs involving other kingdoms. Having control of emotions in these sorts of situations is deceitful and would make us an untrustworthy race.

"Many Spirit Elves actually choose to use their element to benefit us all by becoming a healer. You see, they can not only help you feel better emotionally, but can give healing energy to most injuries, speeding up the recovery rate. I, on the other hand, felt my calling was to train others to be at one with their element – or elements, in your case."

I sighed, wishing he'd use his element to make me feel better right now, as frustration filled me, knowing this element wasn't coming as easily as the others. I was determined to wield it nonetheless.

Wondering what Isaac and Bay were up to, I was surprised when Bay suddenly pushed Isaac backwards. "Don't come near me! The way you treat Thea is appalling. Leave her alone!" he shouted, throwing in a punch.

What the hell was going on? Totally confused, I couldn't believe Bay was going up against the Head Thill guard! Not the most sensible of things to do.

What was he talking about? Isaac and I had gotten a lot closer recently and he was nothing but gentle and kind around me; well, maybe a little overbearing at times, but still.

Isaac then began shouting back, pushing Bay to the ground. This time, both Inwen and I stepped forward, not quite sure what we could do to stop this situation from getting any worse. As they lunged at each other again, I began to panic, thinking someone was going to get seriously hurt, and without thinking I closed my eyes and concentrated firstly on Isaac as he was the stronger of the two. Picturing his face, his breathing and the emotions I felt sure he was feeling at that particular moment, I slowed down my own breathing until it felt like time itself had stopped. It felt completely natural as the energy from my surroundings seemed to infiltrate into my very being, my soul, so much stronger than the energy I used from the other elements. It seemed to still within me, allowing a sense of peace and calm to wash through me, and it was this emotion I tried to push out from within. Holding out my arms in front of me, palms facing outward, I pushed again, harder this time, and closed my eyes to give me greater concentration. With every breath out, so too calm energy projected onto Isaac. As I moved onto Bay, my whole body tingled in awareness as I began to sense the emotions of everyone around me, not just the two boys. It was mind blowing, like I had become one with them.

Focusing on Isaac in particular, his aura seemed to glow as he continued to be awash with the thoughts and energy I was enveloping him with, and in return I felt a warmth, a love he was projecting at me. It was indescribable and left me breathless. Upon opening my eyes, I focused solely on Isaac and reciprocated the look of warmth and desire he was giving me. Then, turning to face the others, I realised how quiet it had become and saw they were all smiling at me...

Instantly suspicious, I asked, "You weren't really fighting, were you?"

Inwen didn't even look the slightest bit remorseful as she said they hadn't; in fact, she started laughing. "We knew the best way of getting you to harness your spirit magic was to get you to think one of your friends was in danger of being harmed."

"What better way to do this than making it look like Isaac and I were going to kill each other?" Bay snorted out, sniggering at my look of indignation.

"I could tell when you were beginning to influence me, it was like my thoughts weren't my own and you were telling me how to feel. Impressive," Isaac said, raising his eyebrows at me.

Later that day Talawen reported back his excitement at hearing my progress, reiterating again how I was becoming a powerful weapon against Minen. Whilst I knew he had absolute confidence in me, it wasn't helping relieve the pressure I was already feeling.

With so much time spent in training, the weeks had sped by far too quickly, until it was only eight weeks until my coronation. Luckily, the guards felt I should be allowed out for good behaviour and so two trips had been planned, one to go out with the twins and the other to finally go and meet Eli's family.

After the excitement of the last time we had gone out, the twins and I decided to play it safe and went to chill out by the lake. The guards were good about keeping a discreet distance so we had some privacy. Even so, we still kept our voices to a whisper when we spoke, due to the subject.

"Our cousin Ryder said the Council are trying to keep the panic to a minimum," Inwen said. "No one knows why the Earth Elves are disappearing, but apparently there are now fifty-eight whose whereabouts are unknown. With so many gone, there has been pressure placed on the Council Elders to immediately hold an investigation, but Minen is still insisting it's a coincidence."

I snorted at the absurdity of it all. Fifty-eight Elves out of thousands might not sound like many, but it was certainly enough that the alarm should be raised. "This has to mean Minen's involved," I said. "Why else wouldn't he want this investigated? It doesn't make sense." I sighed, frustrated I didn't yet have the power to get involved.

"What about talking to Talawen?" Bay suggested.

"I've tried, but he dismissed it, saying I should instead be focusing on getting ready for the coronation. Apparently I have to write a speech now on top of everything else," I groaned, my stomach tying itself into knots at the thought of having to speak in front of thousands of people.

We sat there in silence, watching as a couple of boats drifted by. Neither they nor I could think of anything we could do to help, however frustrating it was. In the end we agreed we'd let each other know if we heard anything more.

CAN I PLAY WITH THE BIG KNIVES?

Feeling subdued from the previous night's conversation, I ended up just picking at my food at breakfast. Both Isaac and Eli sat with me and I could tell they were concerned by my depressed mood and poor eating habits. Thinking it was to do with the impending coronation, they tried to tell me how well I was coming along with my training and that because of the progress I had made I would be starting offensive training today. Although this wasn't the real problem, they did manage to cheer me up as I pictured all the lethal weapons that hung in locked cases around the training room.

Wanting to get started, I got up from the table and practically ran to the training grounds, impatient with

Isaac's slow but steady stride. Eli walked with us so he could speak to one of the professors, and left us with a reminder that we were going to visit his family tonight.

"So which weapons are we going to use first?" I said excitedly, jumping up and down like a little child. Isaac grinned back, bemused by my enthusiasm at handling dangerous weapons.

"Before you even pick up a weapon, you must think about why you are in the position to need one. If someone is coming to attack you, their aim will be to kidnap or possibly kill you. Therefore the most important thing is how you can survive until help arrives. In the meantime, in that situation, knowing the correct stance and your opponent's weakest areas can help save your life."

On board with what he had said, I immediately stood, facing Isaac in my defensive position as I waited for him to continue.

"You need to play to your strengths and know your weaknesses, to help give you the advantage. Your advantage, Thea, is how quick you are, as well as your ability to wield magic, and not just one type. However, when faced with a Goblin or another sort of attacker, they are more than likely going to be taller than you, which will be a weakness for you. What you need to do is get as close to them as possible as it will make it more difficult for them to use their height to their advantage. The other thing to remember is to conserve your energy as much as possible, as you yourself know how tired you become when using your magic."

I nodded.

"Come on then...do your worst," he smirked, raising his eyebrows in challenge and summoning me forward with a flick of his wrist.

Adrenaline coursed through me, knowing I had the chance to pay him back for all the times he had tried to attack me. Grinning, I lunged forward and performed a side kick, hoping to knock him off balance, but all it did was provide him with the opportunity to sweep his right foot out and knock me over.

Seeing the quirk to his mouth as his lips turned upward, I realised he was enjoying this. There was no way I was going to let him win. I tried again, this time driving my palm into his stomach, following through with a knee thrust straight into his abdomen. While there wasn't as much force behind my punches and kicks as I may have liked, I was pleased to hear him release a grunt and topple slightly before righting himself.

I stuck my tongue out at him, gleeful that I was beginning to get the hang of what he was saying. However, I should have known not to provoke him so soon, as suddenly I found myself on the floor with him on top, straddling me. Pinning my arms above my head, he was breathing heavily, his face inches from mine. His hair hung forward over his eyes and as he leaned over; I could feel the heat coming off him in waves. Intoxicated by him, it was all I could do not to groan out loud my desire for him.

At first, neither of us moved, but then slowly his head came closer to mine until our lips were almost touching. I could feel his breath caressing my lips as he looked up into my eyes, trying to read my expression. Oh goddess, I thought, this is it. Holding my breath in anticipation, I lifted my body to meet his, with the aim of getting as close as possible, the desire in both our eyes reaching breaking point. Suddenly the sound of people walking past our room startled him, breaking the spell we were both under.

"I'm sorry...I—" he started before standing up and walking out, closing the door behind him. Breathing heavily, I tried to make some sense of what had just happened. Finally! It wasn't just my imagination. There was something between us. Yes, he was being confusing as hell, but at least I now knew he really liked me! Rolling over, I stood up slowly, deep in thought. Collecting my things, I headed out after him to find my other guards. Looking slightly confused by Isaac's sudden disappearance, they explained his orders: to wait for Eli who was going to continue with my training after lunch.

Realising now wasn't the time to process what had just happened, I tried to calm down as I waited for Eli. When he arrived, he had brought lunch for us. We enjoyed reminiscing over stories from our human lives until it was time to get back to training.

As we gazed at all the different weaponry the room had to offer, Eli filled me in on some more Elf history.

"Just like with elemental magic, Elves have an affinity with a particular weapon," he said, waving his arm around at the assortment of spears, knives, bows, daggers and swords on display.

"How do you know which weapon is right for you?"

"You will just know." He winked at me. "Go on, pick one."

Not understanding, I walked forward, looking at the swords first. There was a huge selection, all of varying sizes, and I tentatively reached for a fairly long looking sword that had intricate designs running along the hilt. Made out of bronze, it was heavier than I thought and didn't sit that comfortably in my hand.

"That's a Makhaira, a Greek sword from ancient times. It is also known as a backsword due to it having a single cutting edge, you see," he said pointing at the edge.

"What's it doing here?" I wondered, reminding him we were in a completely different realm.

"Lots of the swords you see here are from the human realm. We have the Asi from the Iron Age, a Khmali and Curtana from the Middle Ages, right up to the more modern Kalis and Spadroon. Whilst we don't use them to fight in this realm, there are many similarities with Elf designs. The ones along here," he said, pointing to another wall, "are all Elf-made."

It was then that I realised what he meant about knowing which weapon would be right for me, as I began to feel the magic within them calling out to me. I walked forwards, feeling drawn in particular to a set of jewelled daggers and gasped, as when I reached out to touch them their energy moved up through my arm and into the rest of my body. This was different to other energies I'd absorbed. The daggers seemed alive, sharing with me their past, including the battles they had been in. It was as though they wanted me to be a part of them, I thought, as I ran my fingers over the gems, which included rubies, sapphires and diamonds of varying sizes interwoven into the hilts. Turning them over, the daggers felt light and comfortable in my hands, as though they were natural extensions of me. It was like I instinctively knew how to use them.

"Do you feel that?" he urged, seeing my face light up.

I nodded in wonderment.

"These daggers are particularly special as they belonged to your mother, Queen Lina-Driel, and were faithful to only her until her life ended," Eli said quietly, coming up behind me. "It seems only fitting they are now calling out to you."

Feeling suddenly alone, I turned to face him as he drew me into a hug, kissing my forehead. We stood there like that for a while as I processed what he had just said.

I was excited to have found my own daggers. It was nice finally feeling like I had an attachment to something in this world and I was itching to use them. Hopefully I would soon be able to wield them like any accomplished guardian.

Eli also gave me a beautiful bow and arrow carved out of wood from the Forest of Arlain, which he explained was a place blessed by the goddess. It was known to have high levels of magic and so the wood from there was often used, due to the magical qualities the trees held. I would be trained in how to use a bow and arrow with the other students, as all Elves had one. "Your bow string is made for strength and weight, so we use dragon skin for this," he said, pulling back the string.

"What?! Dragons are real?" I exclaimed as Eli laughed at me. I really needed a 101 class in all things Faery!

"You have no idea what's out there, Thea, and half of it you don't want to know!" he chuckled.

Shaking my head, we made our way back to the palace to get ready to go to his parents' house. I felt apprehensive about what they would think of me. Not only had I taken their only son away from them for the past seventeen years, but I also wasn't sure what Eli had told them about me and whether he had mentioned his feelings – romantic, or otherwise. After the almost kiss with Isaac earlier, my feelings for them both were all over the place, but I knew that whatever the outcome, someone was going to get hurt.

THIRTEEN

MEETING THE PARENTS... AND A WHOLE LOT OF TROUBLE

Dusk had fallen by the time we set off, and I was pleased to see Janin and Taro were part of my guard tonight.

Eli grabbed my hand as we walked past Lake Fallowen and down an unfamiliar path. It felt comfortable, but I did still try to pull my hand discreetly from his. He looked at me, frowning slightly, but didn't ask me what was going on, thank goodness. I mean it wasn't like Isaac and I had actually kissed, but somehow I felt like I hadn't been honest with Eli, like I had betrayed him somehow. Trying to push romance from my mind, I started asking him questions about his family.

"So what do your mom and dad do?"

"Mom is a Spirit Elf and decided she was called by the goddess to use this gift to help Elves who are in disputes with each other. Kind of like a human counsellor. You can guess why they are useful in that role."

"Yes of course," I thought aloud. "They would definitely have an advantage at mediating on behalf of others to resolve problems."

"Spirit Elves have to take an oath though, stating they won't influence a situation to either party's advantage, they must stay neutral at all costs," Eli stated, as I recalled what Talawen had told me about not misusing this gift.

"Dad actually works with Council Elder Erwin, working on issues that affect Earth Elves. Therefore, as you can imagine, his job hasn't been easy of late, especially with all the disappearances. Due to his support of Erwin, Minen has made him a target as well but he doesn't care, especially now that you are here. He can't wait to meet you; he's been pestering me since you arrived to meet up. He has the utmost confidence you will bring Aroben back to the kingdom it once was."

Rolling my eyes to hear of yet another Elf who seemed to think I was going to save the kingdom, I was glad to see we had arrived.

The cottage was beautiful. Made completely out of wood, it was nestled in between two small hills, and a stream wound its way past the side of the house, through the gardens and into a nearby river. The garden was awash with flowers of all different colours, shapes and sizes. It was perfect. Such a tranquil and calm setting, I could see why his parents wanted to live here.

"We're here!" Eli called out as he opened the front gate. Hearing a squeal, we were then greeted by a small girl running towards us at top speed. Eli, expecting this response, was bent over, ready to scoop her up in his arms, and swung her around.

"Be careful not to drop her!" a woman scolded as she followed the girl out. The huge smile on her face let me know she wasn't serious and she came to greet us, arms opened wide. Eli went to hug the lady who I was thinking must be his mother, and then turned Kayla towards me. She was a gorgeous little thing, looking tiny in Eli's arms. With long wavy brown hair, she had the same sparkling green eyes as Eli, but these ones also had a mischievous glint in them, confirming my suspicions that she was more than likely a handful.

"Thea, allow me the pleasure of introducing you to my lovely mother, Hana, and the gorgeous and irresistible Kayla," he finished, tickling Kayla until she laughed. "Kayla is five years old!"

Smiling at them both, I held my hand out as Hana shook it. As she then went to bow, I pleaded with her not to. "Really, please don't, I feel like you are family after knowing Eli for so long." He started chuckling, knowing how embarrassed I got with all the attention from my royal status.

"Well, if we are family," Hana replied, "it is only right we hug!" she said, smiling kindly as she pulled me into an embrace. Kayla then got down from Eli's arms and pulled on my hand shyly, leading me into their living room.

"You have a lovely home," I said as Kayla squirmed a little, getting comfortable on my lap.

"Thank you. This house was built with lots of love and hard work. We are very fond of it," Hana said, pleased with my comment. Just then, a man who looked like an older version of Eli walked into the room. I couldn't help but grin at the resemblance between the two.

"So Eli, you have finally brought *the* Thea-Driel to come and meet us," he said, winking playfully at me. I stood up to shake hands with him. "I'm Todan and it's an honour to meet you," he said kindly.

"Likewise," I replied. It was lovely to see this other part to Eli's life that he had had to keep hidden from me for so long, especially as it was clear how important they were to him.

"Well, supper is almost ready, but I wasn't quite sure how many I would be feeding. Did any other guards come along with you tonight?" Hana questioned.

"Three others: Janin, Caleb and..." he said, pausing for a moment as he turned to Kayla, "...Taro is here!" We watched as she squealed, jumping up and down in the process upon hearing the last name in my guard entourage. She then proceeded to run outside to find him as Taro suddenly appeared, scooping her up and swinging her around like Eli had.

"The guards are part of Eli's family and treat Kayla like their little sister," Hana confided to me with love in her eyes. "They have been really good about visiting and keeping in touch while he was away." She smiled at me.

Feeling instantly guilty I started to apologise. "I'm sorry I took him away from you. If I had known—"

"Oh no, please don't apologise," Hana interrupted. "We are so proud of our son and his role in trying to keep you safe from harm. I'm sure you know how important you are. Anyway...he would come home to visit as often as he could."

As she turned to look at Eli, I saw the way she looked at her son and felt a sudden pang of jealousy that I would never experience a mother-daughter relationship again.

"Let's sit outside to eat. The dining table isn't big enough for us all," she laughed as we all made our way outside.

Squashed in between Eli and Janin, we roared at all the stories Hana and Todan told us about when Eli was a boy, laughing even harder when we saw how embarrassed Eli was getting. I aimed to dig him in the ribs but he instead grabbed hold of my hand and kissed it. Then refusing to let go, he put my hand in his lap as he moved a little closer. He continued looking at me with such an intense longing that I blushed.

This display of obvious affection meant it took me a while to realise the table had gone silent, with everyone looking at us expectantly. Taro even snickered, until I glared back at him.

As Hana began to clear the table with Kayla, Taro and Caleb's help, Todan drew me into conversation. "How are you feeling with your impending coronation? I hear from Eli that you have very impressive talents and have been working hard to understand the ways of the kingdom."

"I'm getting there." I fidgeted, the familiar wave of nausea coming back. Eli squeezed my hand in reassurance. Suddenly remembering what Eli had said about who his father worked for, I impulsively asked him about the Earth Elf disappearances, waiting with bated breath as I was not sure how he was going to respond.

Todan didn't actually seem surprised or bothered

by my question, even though Eli and Janin had tensed up.

"We're frustrated more than anything. I don't know if you have heard but the total missing has now reached sixty-four," he said with a sigh. "Finally, Minen has decided to investigate what's going on but he still refuses to address the situation with the kingdom as a whole, making them all fully aware what's going on. The problem with this, though, is that all the secrecy shrouding what's going on is fuelling inaccurate rumours and taking attention away from what we are going to do to address the problem," he grunted, clearly annoyed.

"And no one has any idea where they are being taken? I mean...that's what the Council thinks is happening, don't they? That they're being kidnapped?"

"Yes, and whilst we can't accuse anyone directly until we have proof, it saddens me to say we think someone on the Council is behind the disappearances," he said, giving me a furtive look. Not letting him know that I had already come to the same conclusion and that Minen was my main suspect, I tried to act surprised by the news.

Looking around at the others, I realised I was making them feel uncomfortable and changed the subject again.

"What element can you wield?" I asked.

"Air, like Eli," Todan responded. "Hana wields spirit, as Eli might have already told you, and Kayla's is earth," he said, straining over telling me that last part. I turned to watch Kayla as Taro was chasing her around the garden. Feeling very protective over Eli's sister already, the thought that something may happen filled my stomach with dread.

"It's time to go," Eli whispered.

Sitting up suddenly, I realised I had drifted off, snuggled up against his shoulder. I yawned and then looked around, observing such a happy scene; Hana and Todan were sitting quietly on a loveseat listening to Kayla chat animatedly to them whilst Caleb, Taro and Janin were all competing with each other as they used their elements to make various objects move, with disastrous results. The laughter and camaraderie coming from them made me realise how fond they were of each other, very much like brothers, confirming in my mind what a strong unit the Thill guard actually were – yet another reason why I didn't want to come between Isaac and Eli.

Looking back at Eli, I smiled as he pulled me onto his lap, securing me into his warm embrace. Resting my head in the crook of his neck, I breathed in deeply, feeling content and safe; however, remembering I was playing with his heart and that he could misconstrue us being in this position, I sighed and stood up, walked over to his parents and gave them both a hug goodbye. Thanking them for a fantastic evening, I promised I would come back and visit again soon.

We started to head back towards the palace in a comfortable silence, and realising how dark it was becoming, I grabbed onto Eli so I wouldn't keep tripping over all the tree roots. My other three guards had drawn nearer to Taro to my right, with Caleb and

Janin taking up the rear.

It was after a couple of minutes that intuition suddenly kicked in, along with an unsettling feeling that something was wrong. Pausing, I looked around me, straining to see or hear if there was something out there, at the same time as the guards also realised something was wrong.

Without a moment's hesitation, Eli pulled me behind him, shielding me from the unknown danger as Taro shouted at Caleb and Janin.

"Behind you, move now!" he shouted to the others as a flash of light came towards us. As Eli pulled me down to the ground, I realised the light was actually a flame that had now set a nearby tree alight. At least the light coming from the fire meant that I could see what was going on.

Just then all hell broke loose. I saw Janin, who had seconds before been standing next to me, being thrown at least fifty feet away. Looking around for the source of all the commotion it was then that I saw the four Goblins and two Elves fighting us.

Panic overwhelmed me as I realised how outnumbered we were and I couldn't even see if Janin was okay. Taro and Caleb were trying to take them all on at once whilst Eli scooped me up and flung me over his shoulder. Running faster than should be possible, he ducked and dived through the trees, trying to outrun them; the only sound coming from him was quick breaths.

Feeling disoriented and completely terrified, I gripped on for dear life until a surge of energy split us apart. Flying through the air, I put my hands up just in time, as I smacked into a tree. Screaming, I felt an intense pain shoot through me as my body made impact. Trying to sit up, I pressed my fingers to my ribs tenderly and winced, realising a couple of them had broken. My breathing became laboured and I felt very dizzy as quick hands pulled me flat down to the ground. I started to fight off the attacker until I realised it was Eli.

"Sssh, it's me," he said. "Thea sweetheart, where are you hurting?" he asked, panicking as I began sobbing.

"My ribs hurt and my head and I can't breathe!" I wheezed as I realised one of the broken ribs must have punctured a lung. At that moment someone came out of the darkness, and as he ran towards us Eli took a protective stance in front of me. He looked ready to take on the world as fierce determination shone in his eyes.

"Eli, it's me!" Janin hissed, skidding down to the ground next to us. He was looking the worse for wear with blood smeared on his face, coming from a deep gash on his cheek, and he was also holding his shoulder awkwardly. Even with his obvious injuries, I thanked the goddess he was alive.

"What now?" he directed at Eli.

"Wait...I hear someone!" Eli whispered back as I tried to quiet my breathing. After waiting several minutes I started to move, trying to alleviate the pain that was getting worse. Even with Eli trying to keep me still, my moving was all it took for three of the Goblins who had followed us to realise where we were, and they attacked again.

Standing up to shield me from them, Eli and Janin went on the offensive, using air to push one Goblin into a tree with a sickening crunch. They then both turned in perfect synchronisation to fight the other two.

Dragging myself across the ground, I tried to find a place to hide, knowing there was no way I could run away.

The guards were so focused on what was going on in front of them, they didn't realise an Elf who rivalled Eli in size had come up behind me. Grabbing me around the waist and lifting me up, I screamed as the pain suddenly became unbearable. Weakly, I managed to kick out at him as Eli and Janin turned around, realising what had happened.

"Shit!" Janin shouted as he and Eli moved to stand back to back, now trying to take on the threat from both sides.

Hanging limply in my attacker's arms, I racked my brains trying to think what I could do to get out of this situation.

Remembering how I could now control any of the elements, I closed my eyes and tried to picture myself in a cocoon of protective fire just like I had used when I was attacked in the human world. However, the cut to my head made it difficult to concentrate, along with the sudden motion as my captor began carrying me away from Eli and Janin. My fear took on a new high as I felt sure I was going to die.

Drawing magic from within, I tried once again to relax and concentrated on building up a protective barrier around me.

I knew it had worked when the Elf suddenly dropped me, yelling out in surprise. Looking around, I was astonished to see that not only had I made the flame barrier appear, but I had set the ground and my attacker alight as well.

Not sure which way to head, I stumbled as fast as I could into the darkness, trying to ignore the pain that was threatening to make me pass out. I could sense my barrier had now disappeared, as the last of my energy was now directed on just moving forwards, and hopefully away from the danger.

Thinking I had finally escaped, I didn't realise until it was too late that I had run directly into the path of another attacker. The snarl coming from this latest Goblin caused me to freeze, which was the worst thing I could have done as it gave him enough time to stab me in the stomach. Trying to suck in a breath, I looked down in horror to see blood pouring out of me at an alarming rate.

Thinking this was my time, I slowly sank to the ground, becoming oblivious to the chaos that was still well under away around me. With my head turned to the side I watched in a dream-like state as flames coursed through the undergrowth. It was then I became aware of screams, which stopped suddenly when the head of the Goblin who had stabbed me rolled to a stop nearby. Unsure who had come to my aid, I turned slightly and saw I was inches away from Isaac.

FOURTEEN

DARKNESS DESCENDS

"Thea...Thea! Look at me," he said frantically.

Trying to focus on his handsome face, I lifted the hand that I had held pressed against my wound, trying to touch him. Upon feeling the wetness on my hand, he looked down and realised I had been stabbed. Seeing his face turn ashen I knew it couldn't be good. He pulled off his shirt, ripping it into strips and wrapping them tightly around my stomach. It was all I could do to keep awake as my whole body had taken on a floating, disjointed feel.

"What are you doing here?" I mumbled weakly.

"Taro alerted us back at the palace. The other Thills are out looking for you as well. Come on, you're still not safe and you need help," he said worriedly as his eyes flitted over my various wounds.

"Where's Eli? Are the others okay?" I asked, trying to get up until another wave of pain shot through me.

"Don't move! I'm going to carry you, you're going to be fine," he insisted although I felt he was the one needing reassurance.

I groaned, my head flopping uselessly, and I began to feel even weaker. The loss of blood wasn't helping. Isaac lifted me up carefully, somehow managing to keep one hand applying pressure to my stab wound as he ran determinedly towards the healer centre.

"Hold on Thea, we're almost there," Isaac said soothingly, repeating it like a mantra every now and then.

My head lay heavy on his chest, listening to his soothing words before I began to go under, the events of the night becoming too much to bear.

Moaning softly, I came to, and seeing the sun beginning to rise I realised it was dawn.

Overwhelming relief washed through me, knowing I was in the healer centre, safe and in a warm, comfortable bed. Next to me, Isaac was sitting in a chair with his head inches away from mine. He had fallen asleep still holding my hand. Even in sleep he looked exhausted and I noticed a few cuts and bruises scattered around his face. Running my fingers softly along the contours of his eyes, I was so relieved he had come out of this relatively unharmed.

Isaac woke up with a start, checking my body for

further injuries before looking relieved once he realised I was awake. He stared at me with such a burning intensity I couldn't doubt the love that shone in his eyes. In fact, they held so much emotion I had to look away, until his finger gently turned my chin back towards him.

"You're awake," he said simply. "I thought for a minute we had lost you, that it was happening again."

"What do you mean?" I asked, confused.

"Thea, you must forgive me," he began, the anguish evident on his face.

"I must explain everything to you. I'm the reason your parents died.... I...I was unable to protect them. They were my responsibility...just like with you, I had been personally assigned to keep them safe and I failed. It's happening again...I'm going to lose you too," he said brokenly as he cupped my face in his hands.

"I still keep replaying what happened to them in my head. Things were terrible...there was so much tension in the whole of Aroben as Elves realised the struggle for power between the throne and Council was getting to breaking point. Many had sided with your parents, wanting equality for all, but that still didn't stop Minen."

He paused, trying to gain control of his emotions before continuing.

"We were walking back from the Festival of Lights and everyone was feeling relaxed after all the celebrations. No one had heard anything from Minen for a couple of days and the celebrations had put everyone in a good mood. There were five other guards with us, one of them you know, Janin.

"When we were only five minutes away from the

palace, King Thurindir clutched his head, bending over in agony, and then collapsed to the floor. Realising that it was magic that was torturing him, we looked around trying to see who was causing this."

Isaac looked at me in sympathy. "I'm sorry, I know this is difficult to hear, but it's time for you to know the truth," he said softly.

"The same thing happened to Queen Lina," he continued. "When she collapsed to the ground, we decided the threat was too great to stay out in the open, so, splitting up, we took to different healers just in case we were walking into an ambush. However, before we could act on this, fifteen Goblins and a handful of Elves, some of whom I recognised from the Council, including Elder Lhinanor, attacked us. We were completely overwhelmed and fought our hardest to overcome them, but whatever we tried to do to escape, there were just too many. They made me watch as they tortured the king and queen further before killing them." He sobbed, looking at me in desperation, wanting – needing – me to forgive him. "We lost four men that night as well as our beloved king and queen."

"Thea, I'm so sorry. I understand if you can't forgive me," he said, trying to brush away the tears that were streaming down my face. At that moment I felt so many mixed emotions; crushing anger at how my parents had been made to suffer before they died, and immense sadness at the anguish that was still eating away at Isaac. He hadn't been able to forgive himself.

His grief was unbearable to watch and I reached out, wanting to comfort him. "Isaac, I don't doubt for a second that you did everything you could to save them, and I'm not going anywhere. You can't get rid of me that easily," I teased gently, trying to get him to smile before I continued.

"You have been an incredible guard, Isaac. Considering all the incidents I have been involved in, many self-inflicted," I admitted with a hint of a smile, "you have kept me safe each time."

"I will always be there for you Thea," he whispered as he kissed my hand.

"I need to confess something else as well. When we first met, I could see that flicker of recognition in you...you knew who I was...you had remembered me. You see, ever since you were hidden in the human world, I have been watching you, making sure you were protected, much to Eli's frustration as he felt at first it was because I didn't trust him. But that wasn't the real reason Thea. I've always felt a strong connection to you right from your birth. I couldn't stop thinking about you. At first I was protective of your safety but then over the years it became more than that; I'm in love with you Thea and I can't hide these feelings any longer. You must know how I feel, I need you to be mine," he finished possessively.

Trying to come to terms with the overload of information, I suddenly had flashbacks as I remembered all those times Isaac had been in my life as he said, always in the background, always just watching but always there.

Reaching forward, I ran my fingers through his dishevelled hair, drawing him closer until our lips were just touching. His warm breath, mixed with his heady scent, left me breathless as I leaned forward so that our lips connected. Suddenly, an uncontrollable urge passed through me and I could tell he felt the same as we kissed each other with growing passion. As our tongues met, my hands had a mind of their own as I reached to feel over the contours of his body and, oh my goddess, it was as sculpted and defined as I had imagined. His stubble tickled my face and gave him a rugged look, making him even more appealing.

Moaning, I pulled back slightly to look in his eyes and saw a burning intensity shining back at me. I couldn't get enough of him and tried my hardest to remember that at any minute someone might walk through the door, and that I was lying in a hospital bed! One thing I did know: this felt so right. He was the one my body craved and I couldn't get enough of him. Somehow my body knew I was to be connected to his, we were meant to be together and if he continued to kiss like that, I was never letting him go.

Some while later I realised I felt exhausted again even though I had been asleep not too long ago. Looking into Isaac's crystal blue eyes, I let him know with just a look how much he meant to me, moments before I drifted back off to sleep.

Waking with a start, I realised I must have been asleep all day as it was already dark outside. Wondering what had woken me, I looked around, and realising Isaac must have left. Climbing out of bed, I winced at my still sore body and walked tentatively over to the door. I was about to open it when I heard raised voices in the corridor.

"We've just heard word from Taro. All those involved in the attempted kidnapping are dead but something else has happened...Kayla has gone missing!" Caleb said frantically.

Talawen's calm and authoritative voice then spoke up.

"Where's Eli, does he know?"

"Yes, he's with his parents and Taro now. They are trying to work out what happened. They think she's been taken like the other Earth Elves. Taro wonders if kidnapping Thea was only part of the plan last night, the other being to take Kayla."

Feeling all my strength leave me, I sagged against the wall as my breathing shallowed. This couldn't be happening. Not Kayla, she was too young and innocent. I swallowed down the bile that rose in my throat at the thought of someone harming her.

Hearing movement in my room, Isaac and Talawen rushed in to see me standing there with a shocked look on my face. They realised I had heard what had happened and both tried to muster a blank expression so as not to let me see how worried they actually were.

Picking me up gently, Isaac tried carrying me back to the bed as I fought to be put down. Talawen followed, waiting for the outburst he knew was coming.

"We must do something...this has gone on long enough," I gasped, clutching my stomach as the wound began throbbing again due to all the movement. "Minen has got to be stopped! What are we going to do?!" I insisted, trying futilely to get back out of bed whilst Isaac's iron grip kept me in place.

"Thea calm down. We will do something," Talawen said trying to reassure me. "We already have a few leads as to where the other Earth Elves might be. We are handling this, but we must be careful. If Minen realises we are on to him it will make rescue harder, you must see that," he implored.

Falling back against the pillow, I felt dreadful both physically and emotionally and closed my eyes as another round of dizziness hit me.

Isaac watched on anxiously.

"Thea stop this, you are too weak and need to rest."

I tried to slow down my breathing. "As soon as I'm well, I'm helping. I don't know how, but you can't shut me out...I must do something," I said firmly, looking at Talawen and daring him to say otherwise.

As Talawen left, promising to share any news as soon as he heard, I began to feel vulnerable and more alone than ever. Realising Isaac was planning to leave my room as well, I called out. "Please don't go."

"I won't go anywhere, I was just going to check on Caleb," he murmured, turning to look at me as though I was the most precious being in the world. "I can't stop thinking about you. Your smile, your eyes, your total disregard for your safety..." he smirked. "Everything about you. I love you," he said, kissing me tenderly. The heat and unconditional love burning in his eyes made me want to melt on the spot.

"I love you too," I replied.

Breathing in his heady scent, I waited for him to continue what he'd started. He seemed to know what I was craving and I didn't have to wait long as he bent down to kiss me again, slowly at first until it built into an intensity that seemed to set my whole body on fire.

Pulling away completely breathless, he trailed his fingers, caressing my skin on their way down towards my hip. Being careful not to hurt me, his mouth showered gentle kisses, starting at the sensitive spot on my neck and then slowly moving down towards my chest, only stopping when a small gasp escaped my lips.

"I can't believe you want me!" he said, looking at me with complete awe. "I had thought you and Eli belonged to each other. The other guards and I knew he saw you as something more than just someone to protect. He loves you too, not that he has admitted it to you yet."

"Eli has been such a steady presence in my life, both here and back in the human world. His friendship has gotten me through such difficult times.... I...I'm not sure I would have survived without him. But with you...I feel like my soul has been searching for you. And now I've found you. You bring me a sense of peace and happiness whenever I'm around you. I didn't realise at first and mistook your abruptness for something else. But now I know. You are meant to be in my life and not just as my guard." I smiled at him, brushing my fingers sensually over his lips.

"Yes, I know I have a lot to make up for," he said sheepishly. "My behaviour was very confusing at first. I just didn't know how to cope with my feelings for you. I thought it would be easier to keep you at a distance but I just couldn't...I couldn't get you out of my thoughts and as time wore on I couldn't help the way I reacted to you. Then it just became too hard not to say anything." Reaching down to seek out my mouth again, he kissed me, bringing warmth and comfort with his touch, and it wasn't long before we were lost in our embrace.

FIFTEEN

CLAUSTROPHOBIA...YOU HAVE NO IDEA

Even with Healer Talawen's help, I had been in the healing centre for three days due to the severity of my injuries. Isaac had stayed with me most of the time, only leaving to shower or attend security briefings with Talawen and the other Council members. Minen told them how shocked he was at my attempted kidnapping, of course, but then bizarrely insisted my security detail be increased. I had no idea what game he was playing but for once Isaac agreed with him: at least he truly wanted to keep me safe.

Whilst recuperating in the healer centre, Taro told me that panic was spreading throughout the kingdom as news about what had happened to me became common knowledge. Many – and not just the Earth

Elves now – were also beginning to worry about their own safety, as Elves of all affinities were now going missing.

There had been no news about Kayla, and although Eli had come to visit me once, it wasn't for long as he needed to get back to search for his sister. I promised him we would find her. I just hoped I could keep that promise. I knew I also had to tell him about Isaac and sooner rather than later, but the timing just sucked. There was also a part of me that was putting it off as I didn't want to cause problems between them both. At least Isaac had agreed I should be the one to talk to Eli about our relationship.

Bay and Inwen had also been keeping me company. Bay tried to cheer me up with all his silly anecdotes about what he had been up to at training, but it wasn't working. I just couldn't seem to get out of the funk I was in, and lying in bed staring at the walls all day was just making it worse. By the fourth day I told Healer Farwen and Talawen in no uncertain terms that I was well enough to be checked out, which is exactly what I did. Isaac wasn't happy about this but knew it was useless to argue with me.

As we walked slowly back to the palace, giving me time to build up my strength again, I got him to fill me in on any other developments with the disappearances. While there wasn't much news, he did tell me they thought the Elves were possibly being kept near a set of mountains about twenty miles away. Eli and a group of Thanes – kind of like the FBI from the human world – were investigating this new lead, however so far they hadn't discovered anything else of help.

The following couple of weeks were difficult as everyone was still so tense. I now had six guards following me around, which was nothing short of claustrophobic, but I put up with it, knowing they were only there to protect me. Even with the increased number of Thills, Isaac was determined to try and get back to some sort of normality for me, and with that and the fact that my injuries had almost healed, I went back to training. I hadn't forgotten my impending coronation and the training I had to complete.

It was on my way to an elemental lesson that Eli came to join my intimidating crew and I. Giving me a huge hug, I squeezed him back just as hard. Looking up I could see in his face the strain he was under – his eyes had a sunken look about them and, judging by the length of his stubble, he hadn't shaved for at least a week or more.

"Still no news?"

"No." He sighed wearily, running his hands through his hair. "We thought we had found out where they were being kept but the lead turned out to be bogus. So instead I decided it was about time I came to see you!" he tried to enthuse. Seeing the look of desire he was giving me, I realised it was now or never. Grabbing hold of his arm, I pulled him off the path we were on and turned towards him, making sure the guards wouldn't be able to hear us. Fortunately Isaac wasn't assigned to me that afternoon.

"Eli, I feel terrible that I have to tell you this, but there's something you should know," I whispered softly. The look of concern he was giving me made me talk quicker, desperate to tell him what I'd done.

"I kissed Isaac. I'm with him...I love him," I blurted out. "I didn't mean to tell you like this, I mean...I wanted to talk to you before anything happened, I didn't know if you liked me like that, I wanted to ask you...but I met Isaac. He told me he used to watch over me, that he told you not to say anything," I trailed off, biting my bottom lip and waiting for his response.

Glancing up at him, I saw his tortured expression as he absorbed the news. The silence that followed was becoming unbearable as I waited for him to say something back.

"How...how did it happen? What about us? You must know how I feel about you?" he implored. "I was going to talk to you. You haven't given us a chance. Please, give me – give us a chance!"

Feeling terrible, I looked down. "Eli, you mean so much to me, but please don't ask this of me. I didn't plan for this to happen, it just did. I didn't mean to hurt you," I said, feeling like the worst person in the world.

"No, I don't want to hear it," Eli called out brokenly, turning around and walking away from me.

Reaching out, I tried to pull him back. "Please don't go!" I pleaded. "I need you...I need you in my life," I finished selfishly.

Turning back to face me, he grabbed me by my upper arms. "This isn't over, Thea. I'm going to fight for you," he said, kissing me fiercely on the lips.

Totally shocked by what had just happened, I watched him walk away before sneaking a look back at my guards to see if they had just witnessed what had happened. Judging by the blank expressions they were trying to fix on their faces, the answer was yes. Great. This was further confirmed by the mischievous wink Janin gave me.

"Someone's in trouble!" he chuckled as we continued walking.

Sighing, I nodded in total agreement. How could

this mess get any worse?

Luckily, on arrival at the grounds I was greeted by the twins as well as Tharlin and Logan, who were pleased I was finally well enough to come back to training. Pulling Inwen to one side, I filled her in on what had happened with Eli. She already knew that Isaac and I were together.

"He did what?!" she exclaimed.

"I know," I yelped back. "He kissed me! In front of the guards as well, and then said he wasn't going to stop fighting for me."

"What are you going to do?" She giggled as I groaned.

"I don't know! He wouldn't listen to me. When Isaac finds out, all hell will break loose. This is exactly what I didn't want to happen – their friendship to suffer because of me," I wailed. "How are things going with you and Logan?" I continued, wanting to change the subject.

"We're still great!" she sighed happily, as we walked over to join them. "Even Bay seems to be coming to terms with us being together."

"How did you achieve that?!"

"Well, Bay came to the conclusion that as Logan is one of his best friends, it might as well be him who dates me instead of a loser that Bay doesn't like. His words, not mine!" She smiled, shaking her head at his over-protectiveness.

Class today was going to be an interesting one as we were focusing on race relations amongst the Faey. Finally I would find out what other races there were apart from Goblins and dragons. Professor Pellam waited for silence before he began.

"As many of you know, the Faery realm doesn't just

consist of Elves. Many other creatures share this world with us. Why is it then that we don't see many other magical beings here in Aroben, other than Elves?" he questioned.

"A treaty thousands of years ago was established to stop the continual fighting that had broken out between the different races over who owned what land," Callon said, surprising me as he stared in my direction, mixed emotions warring on his face. "The treaty ensured that land in Faey was split fairly into different kingdoms so that each race was treated equally. The purpose therefore being that we would all live in harmony with each other. Now as a general rule, most Faey like to keep to their own land. We obviously still mix with other supernatural species that are nearby, but most keep to themselves, living on their land and away from us."

"Excellent Callon," Pellam said approvingly. "And did it work? Do all Faey live in harmony?" he asked, looking around.

"Yes and no," Logan said. "Some races got greedy and weren't satisfied with what they had been given. They caused much unrest in the different kingdoms as they tried to get their own way. Others such as the Gnomes didn't want their own specific piece of land, preferring to live amongst other races, such as with us," he continued.

Surprised at hearing that, I looked around, almost expecting one to suddenly appear in front of me.

"The Nymphs are another race who prefer to be amongst other races even though they have their own kingdom. In fact, they are a race very similar to us as they also are elementals and follow a way of life like us. They are a beautiful race and often seek residence amongst the rivers or trees, which we obviously have in abundance. Although they are a shy race, we have united together when times have required it, such as to fight with us in wars."

"Don't forget there are also some species of Faey that have chosen to live in the human realm, preferring their company. The Brownies and Pixies in particular can be found all over the United Kingdom, especially Devon, Cornwall and parts of Scotland."

As we all sat with rapt attention, Professor Pellam continued.

"Let's go back to what Logan said at the beginning, about the unrest some Faey races have caused. Who are we talking about exactly?"

It was Bay who spoke up this time. "The Goblins are the worst," he said looking at me.

"Yes, their attacks on our royal family have meant they've became firm enemies of ours," Pellam said also turning to me. "Whilst this must be difficult for you Thea, and anyone else here who has lost a loved one by their hand, you need to understand why they attacked us in the past. You see, Goblins are very greedy creatures, spending most of their time searching for jewels and other treasure wherever they can find them.

"When the treaty was signed, all races seemed happy with the land they had been given. The Faey Council, which was and still is made up of a representative from each race, made sure everyone had the same amount of natural and finite resources available for them to do with as they wished. But after some time had passed, the Goblins realised that here in Aroben we had a huge resource of minerals they wanted, in particular gems, which we discovered in the mountains to the south-east of here. This angered the

Goblins greatly, who said they wanted their share of what we had. They felt they hadn't received what was rightfully theirs back when the treaty was outlined.

"Thousands of years have passed since then and still the Goblins aren't happy and have tried to get other magical creatures to support them. Needless to say, many don't want to get involved with them as they are known to be evil and malicious in their dealings with others. The only race that will openly go near them are the Trolls."

"Yeah, well they are too stupid to know not to get involved," Bronid snorted.

"Be careful making comments like that. Trolls may appear slow and dim-witted, but they are actually very calculating and will only intervene if they can personally gain from the deal. Trolls are very unsociable creatures though, so you will rarely see them working together in groups.

"I should also mention that in the past, Goblins have been known to be employed by some members of the Elf community for their own selfish gain."

No need to guess who he was talking about, I thought, as an image of Minen popped into my head. I had seen evidence of this first hand.

"Goblins will do anything for anyone if the payment is in gems," Pellam finished.

Reeling from what I had just heard, I now understood how Minen was able to control them as he had.

The twins and I walked over to our archery class together. As this was my first class, I was a little apprehensive, yet excited at the same time. Apparently using a bow and arrow was something every Elf learned and all are accomplished in this as we'd been gifted with this skill from the goddess Elebrin. It was therefore one of the oldest types of weaponry Elves used, Isaac had told me. Because I had come into this type of training much later than everyone else, it was Janin who had the task of getting me caught up with the others.

"As magic flows through you and into your arrow, you will need to harness that energy as well as your instinct as an Elf, to get the arrow to fall on the intended target. There are obviously other things you need to take into consideration when aiming such as the wind, humidity and temperature, which you can feel by just closing your eyes. Imagine the arrowhead piercing your target," he finished unhelpfully.

On seeing my exasperated face, Bay chipped in with another bit of advice. "The arrows you will be using are footed arrows. They contain two types of wood found in the Forest of Arlain so they'll be lighter and more flexible for you to use. You'll be fine."

Wanting to prove myself, I focused on one of the targets the professor had set up for practice, which was about a hundred yards away. After concentrating for a couple of minutes, I let my body relax and cleared my mind as Janin had suggested. As my breathing slowed, I felt my magic begin to surface and pushed it down through my arm and into the arrow I had poised. The only way I can describe the feeling was that it was as if the magic was being pulled taut within me and was about to snap. At that exact moment I pictured the target in my mind, took a couple of deep breaths and released the arrow, praying I would be vaguely near the target.

The whooping noises I heard from my friends was the reassurance I needed to open my eyes. Realising I had indeed hit the target, I smiled to myself, pleased with my success. My next goal would be to shoot a lot quicker as there was no way I could be this slow if I wanted to use the bow to defend myself. Janin gave me a pat on the shoulder in encouragement.

"Good," he said. "If you want to see a skilled archer at work then you need to look no further than Inwen!" he exclaimed. "She's a master at this and can hit a target over a thousand square yards away," he said impressed, nodding in her direction.

Turning to watch her, I saw what Janin meant as she was hitting targets accurately at least three times the distance of mine, as though she were doing it in her sleep.

At lunch time it was great to have a 'normal' conversation with the others. We spoke a lot about what we would all be doing once basic enlightenment training had finished. It was common to continue with schooling, taking electives to become a specialist in particular areas. Inwen hadn't completely made up her mind what she wanted to do, but was leaning towards becoming involved with the Faey Council and inter-kingdom diplomacy, which I thought was a great idea – partly as, once I led Aroben, we would then see more of each other than I'd originally expected, and also because of her fierce determination to see justice for all. Inwen's relationship with Logan was also on her mind, as they had become so close. It was obvious they were meant for each other but she didn't want to be too far away from him. Fortunately for her, both Logan and Bay had decided they wanted to become Thill guards, and although it would take a further three years of training, they would be near her as they'd be guarding me.

As lunch drew to a close, I couldn't stop the excitement I was feeling, knowing Isaac had squeezed in a further training session to finish off the day. I was definitely looking forward to getting physical with him, and once I'd arrived at the gym, seeing him shirtless with his toned physique on display, I couldn't hide the grin that was plastered on my face. He had obviously just been working out as there was a sheen of perspiration over the exposed parts of his body, making his muscles even more defined.

Upon seeing me, he stalked over with a look that had me quivering inside. Immediately I was hit with his unique musky scent, mixed with sweat, and my breath quickened as he leant down to kiss me, staring intently into my eyes. Leaning forward to try and close the distance even more, there was soon nothing between us as our bodies touched and seemed to meld into one. I slowly brought my arms up around his neck as our lips finally met, trying to explore each other with a sense of urgency. The kiss was so intense it set my soul alight and we both gasped, feverish and frantic to touch each other as much as possible. Running his hands lower down my back, he caressed every part of me, sending shivers and tingles down my spine as waves of pure pleasure washed through me.

"I've missed you," he panted, pulling away for a moment to catch his breath.

"And I you," I replied, desperate to establish that much needed link again between the two of us. We shared another kiss, and once again my body responded to Isaac. We were made for each other, this much I knew.

A while later I pulled back slightly to gaze at the man that meant so much to me. I enjoyed his touch as he gently stroked his thumb across my now tender lips, causing goose bumps to creep up my neck, and my whole body shivered in delight.

Groaning internally, I remembered I had to tell him about my disastrous conversation with Eli, however much of a mood killer it would be, and believe it or not, my conscience was telling me to do it now, especially as it was quite likely they would bump into each other again soon. Taking a deep breath, I plunged straight in.

"I spoke to Eli and it didn't go well," I started, waiting for his reaction.

"Define 'well'," he replied stiffly, his whole demeanour changing with my new topic of conversation. Not that I could blame him, I just didn't want to hide this from him any longer than I already had.

"He said he wasn't going to give up on me. He's going to fight for me," I whispered, trembling slightly as I held my breath.

To my astonishment Isaac started laughing. "I wouldn't expect anything less from him, and he can try!" he said, looking completely unbothered about what I had just said. This was so not the response I had been expecting.

"No!" I panicked. "You can't fight each other, you're friends...f-family," I stuttered. "I won't come between you."

"Don't worry about it," he said dismissively, rubbing my arms soothingly as he saw my distress.

Obviously not wanting to talk about it any further, he broke away and switched back into teacher mode, determined for me to learn further ways to protect myself. Still not believing it had been that easy to tell him, I realised I needed a serious girl talk. Where was Inwen when I needed her?

The main focus of this lesson was to improve my skill with the daggers I had chosen, and I could see he was already pleased with my natural ability in wielding them. Today Isaac used a dirk as his weapon of choice to fight against me, explaining that it was a knife used back in the human world in naval hand-to-hand combat.

"Balance!" he shouted as I stumbled slightly after performing a slash attack. He took this as an opportunity to again explain how important my footwork would be in any battle, no matter what weapon I was using. Rolling my eyes back at him, I wiped the sweat off my forehead, muttering about the way he went on sometimes.

"I've got a surprise for you!" He grinned wickedly as I got ready for another round of sparring. I was exhausted as we had been going at this for a couple of hours, but I wasn't going to complain as he'd probably make me go for longer to make a point.

"It's time to see what you would do if there were two of us attacking you at once. Especially as I think you're becoming too familiar with my fighting style."

Snorting at this change of events, I looked around just as the double doors opened and Taro strolled in, wearing an equally mischievous grin.

"Taro!" I exclaimed in delight. "Come to learn how to fight a princess?!" I teased, flicking my daggers up and down nonchalantly. This was going to be good.

"Let's see what you can do with two combatants!" he replied speculatively, eyebrows raised.

My heart began to thump wildly at the thought of what was coming, and adrenaline gave me a much needed boost as I swung my arms around, trying to stretch out the kinks in my neck. Bouncing on my toes, I started to back up, and swapped my daggers for two swords, knowing I needed something larger, especially as they would both be fighting with swords.

Taro looked clearly delighted at having the opportunity to fight me, and had a glint in his eye as he started to move to the right, watching me like I was some sort of prey and he was the predator. Giving Isaac a look to see what he was doing, I watched as he pulled his own sword out, the one that was usually sheathed behind his back.

Realising I needed to play to my strengths, I knew I was going to have to rely on my elemental magic as well as my fighting skills, even though Isaac hadn't intimated this. I knew there was no other way I could take on two trained Thill guards. Looking at them both moving like warriors, I did for a moment think I should just make a run for it.

"Thea," Isaac said calmly. "If you are attacked, it's very unlikely there will just be one of them. You need to expect this," he said casually as he too began to move towards me, but from the left side.

It was Taro who lunged first, and as he did I used my affinity with air to help me jump up and perform a front flip over their heads, landing behind them. Before having any chance to rejoice at what I thought was a great kick-ass move, Isaac turned in the same moment, bringing his sword up towards my face as it clashed with mine just in time. Staggering back I twisted, ready to defend myself against Taro, who was coming at me, wearing a fierce look of determination.

Remembering it was more of an advantage for me to be nearer my opponent due to my height, I ran towards him, surprising him as I slammed my elbow into his chest. While he was temporarily winded, I focused on Isaac, giving him a hook kick to the leg and managing to bring him down to the floor. Not believing my luck, I wiped the hair that had become plastered to my face and shifted from one foot to another, breathing heavily. Seeing the resolute looks on both their faces, I knew I was now in trouble.

Backing up slightly, I didn't have to wait long as this time they both lunged for me at the same time. Isaac spun around, kicking me in the stomach before I had a chance to move out of the way. I fell to my knees, completely winded. Some boyfriend he was, I thought to myself as Taro then proceeded to punch me in the shoulder, causing me to fall backwards. I grunted as I smacked back into the floor.

Refusing to be beaten, I jumped up with a burst of energy and, acting out of instinct, pushed my spirit energy into them both, making them go temporarily blind. Ha! I thought smugly as I heard their cries of surprise. This was an idea I had been wanting to try after I had accidently done this to myself one night.

Both completely froze, straightening in response and bringing their swords closer to their bodies, trying to protect themselves from the next attack. Laughing at my good fortune and unusual abilities, I decided to put them out of their misery and released them from the darkness they were experiencing – after a few pokes first, of course. The look of awe on both their faces told me they hadn't even considered I could do that to someone.

"Wow Thea, those are some pretty impressive abilities you've got floating around in there!" Taro said, clearly delighted.

"You really are a force to be reckoned with," Isaac chuckled, as he came over to check that he hadn't hurt me too badly. Reassuring him I was fine, he drew me into his warm embrace.

SIXTEEN

THE PREPARATIONS

Waking up slightly stiff and sore from the previous day, I walked down to breakfast. Rubbing my stomach distractedly, I wasn't sure if I could eat anything due to the nerves that had taken up permanent residence in me. You might think I seemed to have a nervous disposition but the coronation was so close now I could smell it – literally: the chefs were preparing the menus for the banquet. Other signs of my impending doom – err, 'big day' – were evident in all the decorations that were being hung around the palace. I had to admit, though, they did look beautiful, as silk drapes in blue and silver were hung from the ceilings and banners with the royal emblem were fixed high up on the walls. Pedestals with the most beautiful exotic looking flowers were also standing to attention every couple of yards or so, in anticipation of the big day.

The most impressive room – and my favourite – was definitely the Great Hall. Even without the extra furnishings it was striking. Standing at approximately a thousand yards, the abundance of light shining into the room was partly a result of the large bay windows, which ran along the entire length of each wall. There were also twelve chandeliers as well as hundreds of miniature lamps placed strategically around the hall that, when lit, certainly made you feel like you were in a fairy tale. My favourite bit about the room was the painted ceiling, which depicted key events from Elf history: battles won and lost, the goddess Elebrin, Lake Fallowen and kings and queens from the past, including, of course, my parents. It might sound corny, but seeing them up there made me feel like they would somehow be watching over me on my big day. I could have stared at their painting for hours. Yes, the Great Hall was definitely a perfect setting for the coronation and Winter Ball.

The rest of the kingdom was also getting ready. Inwen explained that the Winter Solstice Ball was the highlight of the year, and adding my coronation, everyone was in full-out party mode. Inwen was even more excited than most as I had asked her to be my Lady-in-Waiting, an honour that the future queen could bestow on anyone of her choosing. Naturally I chose her and she said yes straight away, easily swayed by the knowledge she would have a dress designed and made for her, as well as the fact that she would have such an important role on the day.

I wished I was looking forward to the day a bit more. Don't get me wrong, I knew my duty, and, as queen, would whole-heartedly do everything in my power to protect the kingdom, especially after everything that had happened recently, but speaking in front of so many Elves was not something I was going to enjoy. I mean, who would want to be on display like that? And it wasn't even as if I would have a speech prepared for me. No, apparently I had to write something that came from the heart. That's what I was supposed to be doing this morning with Talawen – that and attending a special Council meeting that would run through the events of the day. As it included security, all the Thill guards as well as heads from various other enforcements, including representatives from the Thanes, would also be there.

It was Minen who would be leading this meeting and I hoped I'd be able to keep my cool. I didn't know it was possible to despise and hate a man so much. At least he couldn't grumble at my enlightenment progress reports. Now that I had finally passed – and just in time, I might add – there was nothing standing in the way of my officially becoming queen. All the professors had written me glowing testimonies, with Professor Gonan only highlighting my affinity with fire, as agreed. I did feel a sense of self-achievement knowing I had managed to pass in four months and was enjoying the benefits of the enlightenment, including feeling stronger as well as being able to wield the elements in a more controlled and effective way.

My thoughts shifted back to breakfast and I felt some sort of relief knowing Isaac said he would meet me there before all my meetings. However, upon entering the dining room, that soon changed. Coming to an abrupt halt, I saw Eli and Isaac standing inches away from each other in the middle of a heated argument. Judging by the amount of testosterone flying around the room, there was no question as to what they were talking about. Frustration took a hold of me as I groaned to myself. Why did they have to have that discussion today of all days?

Running towards them, I wasn't quite sure how I was going to stop the fight that was clearly brewing.

"Hey, what's going on?" I yelled out in a strangled voice, trying to get in between. This, however, proved to be a futile effort due to how much bigger they were than me. I hardly moved them at all.

"Everything is fine, Thea," Eli said, arms folded as he continued to glare at Isaac. "We were just talking about taking someone else's property without asking!"

"Show me the paperwork to prove the property is yours," Isaac scoffed back.

Listening to their juvenile conversation, I became madder by the minute, realising I was the 'property' they were discussing. Who did they think they were?!

Looking around I expected the guards who were assigned to me that morning to jump in and stop them, but no. Leaning against the wall, clearly relaxed, they were all watching on in amusement. Catching my eye, Janin could see I was annoyed they weren't doing anything.

"Come on Thea, we all knew this was coming, just leave them to it!" He smirked.

Seeing they were going to be no help whatsoever, I stalked back to the two idiots. "I am not a piece of property and I will be with whomever I please!" I retorted angrily, whilst trying to muster up as much authority in my voice as possible.

Completely ignoring me, they continued.

"I've been there for Thea her whole life. I'm the one who was with her at all the highlights in her life as well as the sad times. I know what's best for her. She feels safe with me. I'm her family."

"She feels safe with me too!" Isaac growled back. "Thea means more to me than anything, I'm not giving her up!"

"I'm not giving her up either! I'm going to fight for her. She'll see what a mistake she has made, don't you worry!"

"Hello, I'm right here!" I waved, trying to get their attention. "Don't I get a say in what I want?"

Caleb then began laughing at what I had just said. Turning to him, I gave him a dirty look that threatened violence, and he put his hands up and tried to back away. Eli just cracked his knuckles ominously, continuing to regard Isaac with a look of contempt.

Getting more and more frustrated, I used air to blast them apart and smirked as I was the only one left standing. Before they could retaliate, my prayers were answered as Talawen and Elder Erwin walked into the room with bewildered expressions – clearly they had heard what the two guards were shouting at each other. Luckily for them, my actions had brought the two guards back to their senses as they suddenly realised what they were doing and the audience they had gained.

"Eli, we wanted to go over the latest disappearance reports with you, that is, if you're not too busy?" Erwin inquired, raising his eyebrows.

"Yes of course, I'm just coming," he replied, giving me a sheepish look.

"And Thea," Talawen continued, "I thought we could make a start on your speech before the Council meeting. We should be finished in about half an hour, if you want to come up to my quarters then?"

"Thank you Talawen," I said, grateful to him for more than just the meeting. I knew he realised what had been going on.

Refusing to hang around and talk to Isaac – or any of the other guards for that matter – I walked past them all, head held high. However, it wasn't long before Isaac caught up with me, trying to grab my hand. By this point we had reached the courtyard.

"Thea, my behaviour was appalling, I'm so sorry," he started to say.

"Yeah, you think?" I replied, my voice shrieking as it came out a couple of octaves higher than normal. "I was so embarrassed. I've got so much going on at the moment, I don't need this," I said exasperatedly, crossing my arms before I marched away from him.

Finally, catching up, he pulled me towards him until our faces were inches apart. "Really Thea, I'm sorry," he whispered again, as the intensity in his eyes seemed to make them glow a brilliant, sapphire blue.

Leaning forward, his lips gently brushed mine, waiting to see if I would refuse him. Not that I was about to tell him, but it was all I could do not to pounce on him then and there. Everything in my body yearned for his touch, like he was calling me. I couldn't resist him, however mad I was with him. Letting his spicy, intoxicating smell envelop me, our bodies moulded together, foreheads touching, and I tried to snuggle further into his arms, his warm breath tickling my neck.

"Peace offering?" he asked, pulling an apple from behind him. Giving him one last withering look, I chomped down on the apple before it was time to go see Talawen.

Not wanting Isaac to chance a meeting with Eli again so soon after their last encounter, I told Isaac I would meet him later at the Council meeting, so with my guard in tow, we walked upstairs. I left them in Talawen's office so I could have a few minutes' privacy in the restroom nearby. It was then, en route that I got that gut feeling again telling me to be cautious of whoever was ahead. Not wanting to be seen, I stopped before turning round the corner, instead trying to listen in on the hushed conversation ahead of me.

Realising I knew those voices, I peered around the corner confirming it really was Callon and his father, Elder Lhinanor. They were obviously having an intense and none-too-happy conversation as Callon stared at his father, his face full of venom.

"You have got to try harder!" Lhinanor hissed. "This is not acceptable. You have had plenty of opportunities to be alone with her, to get her to confide in you and become her ally. Time is running out. We must play our part for the greater good!"

"I can't! You might as well make me the one holding a knife to her throat. You must ask someone else," Callon implored. Even from my hiding spot, I could see his hands were shaking and he now looked terrified.

"You will do what I've asked. You've only got a week until the coronation, that's it. One week. If you don't perform so help me—" Lhinanor spat, pushing

Callon with such force his head smacked loudly as it hit the wall.

Callon just stood there as Lhinanor walked away. I too stood still, reeling from what I had just heard. I was sure what they were discussing was about me and it didn't sound good. However, not wanting the guards to come looking for me, I hurried back to Talawen's office, unsure of what to do next.

Trying to concentrate and write a speech, especially after what I had just overheard, was nearly impossible, but Talawen, who had put my twitchy behaviour down to what had happened at breakfast, was being sympathetic and pretty much wrote it himself. Fortunately my speech wasn't too long and there was only a small part I needed to learn off by heart – where I repeated in Elven the oath of Aneyiln, in which I swore I would rule over the kingdom with fairness and justice, so Talawen gave me a copy to practice.

I decided not to mention the conversation I had overheard in the corridor. I didn't know why, but I did know we couldn't confront them, as we had no evidence. At least if something was going to happen I could be slightly prepared.

As we walked together to the Council meeting, Talawen brought up the subject of Eli and Isaac.

"Please do not take offence at my interference, but I just wanted to check Eli and Isaac weren't causing you too many problems? You see, I know I'm not your father but I would hope you feel you could talk to me…if you needed to."

"Thank you. I know…I'm really hoping they will sort it out," I mumbled, feeling a little uncomfortable that even more attention was being directed at me. Fortunately at that moment we arrived at the entrance to the meeting room, which meant we dropped the subject. Taking my seat at the large oval table, I looked around expectantly and it wasn't long before we were ready. Seeing Minen stand up ready to start, I sat up straighter whilst he waited until everyone's attention was directed at him.

"Welcome," he started, looking around at the twenty or so Elves gathered. "As you are aware we are holding this Council meeting today to discuss the happy occasion of Thea's coronation, as well as the Winter Solstice Ball. Isaac, as Head Thill, are the security procedures all in place?"

"Yes," Isaac replied. "All twenty members of the Thill guard will be protecting Thea-Driel on that day. Whilst many of these guards will be placed strategically in various positions around the palace, there will always be six guards with her at all times: Eli, Janin, Taro, Caleb, Dranid and myself."

"Excellent!" he exclaimed loudly, making me jump. "Knowing Thea will be kept safe is so reassuring." He smiled, looking down at me.

Oh please! I thought, as I gave him a sarcastic smile back. Surely no one was buying what he had to say? However, as I glanced around, I realised most of the Elders were.

As talk moved on to the dignitaries that would be coming not only from this kingdom, but all over Faery, I began to switch off and eventually after what must have been three or four hours, everyone stood up to leave. Feeling a sense of relief that I had gotten through this never-ending day without further incident, I neared my guards, watching closely to see how Eli and Isaac were behaving towards each other. True to their word they were acting as if nothing had happened, which I was more than happy to go along with myself. I would just have to wait and see if this really was a long-term arrangement or not.

Just as we were about to leave, Talawen came over, wanting to speak privately to Eli, Isaac and myself.

"Thea, you must be extra vigilant during the next few days," he murmured. "Minen is being far too cooperative about ensuring your security is paramount and he is refusing to comment on the fact that in two days' time he will be handing over the running of the kingdom to you. Something's not right," he finished gravely.

"Eli and I feel the same," Isaac said, as Eli nodded in agreement.

I almost brought up the conversation I had overheard between Callon and his father, but once again something stopped me. I decided to talk to the twins instead and found the perfect opportunity to do so the following day.

Early morning, the twins and Logan were coming over to the palace for two reasons. Firstly, Inwen and I had an appointment with the seamstress who was in charge of making our dresses for the big day, and secondly Bay and Logan had come to do some guard training with Caleb and Taro.

After agreeing to meet the boys later for lunch, Inwen and I walked into an unfamiliar room that looked very much like a sitting room. Nalis, the seamstress, and her team were already waiting. After much previous poking and prodding, today was going to be the final fitting. Inwen helped me into my dress with Nalis' help, but not before making me promise to keep my eyes closed first. The suspense was killing me, as the last time I had seen the dress it was just a pile of strips that had been pinned to me.

"Okay, we're ready," Inwen said breathlessly, as she got more and more excited.

Opening my eyes, I looked in astonishment at the girl staring back from the huge gilded mirror I had been placed in front of. I looked beautiful. In a long royal blue dress that hugged me in all the right places, tiny diamonds had been intricately sewn all over the dress, including along the train that flowed out behind me. The effect of the tiny crystals was certainly impressive as, when I moved, they made the dress shimmer, catching the light beautifully.

Thrilled with how gorgeous it looked on me, I turned to Inwen to see her form-fitting dress was a lighter shade than mine, minus the train and jewels. Together, the dresses complemented each other well. At least we would look the part if nothing else.

After thanking Nalis for all her efforts, we walked to the lake to meet Bay and Logan. Once there I filled them in on the conversation I had overheard between Callon and his father, and asked them what they thought it meant. After they got over their initial shock at the severity of what they had been saying, even though we didn't know if they were talking about me, they were surprised Callon was so unwilling to help his father due to the reputation he had.

"They must have been talking about you!" Bay concluded. "Thea, this is serious. Even if you don't have any proof you must tell Isaac at least," he pleaded, trying to get me to see reason.

"Isaac's got enough on his mind and I can just about put up with all the protection procedures in place at the moment. Telling him what I heard will only make him overreact even more than he already is about my safety," I insisted. "I can't have even more guards following me around!"

"Thea, you must do something," Inwen implored. Obviously they were going for a tag team in trying to persuade me.

"I have...I've already told you three," I said patiently. "All I'm asking is that you help me keep an eye on Callon. Please?"

"Ok, but any strange behaviour from him or his dad and we're telling Isaac and Eli," Bay threatened.

"Agreed." However, they still looked uncertain, unsure if they had made the right decision.

My last evening as a princess was spent taking a walk with Isaac – just the two of us – after what had been another busy day. It was just what I needed.

"It's so beautiful here," I exclaimed, looking around at the Forest of Arlain. The trees seemed to thrum, responding and connecting to the magic within me. I lay down to look up at the stars, which seemed extra bright that night, shining almost as though they knew the importance of tomorrow. I sighed happily, feeling completely at peace.

Suddenly Isaac leaned over me, supporting his weight on his hands as he gently lowered himself down. The look of love he gave me made my toes curl, and I reciprocated his look, watching as his hair flopped into one of his eyes. Leaning back to one side, he pulled me closer, making sure our bodies still touched.

"You are amazing," he said softly as his eyes sparkled. "Tomorrow will be a turning point, bringing the changes we desperately need to bring Aroben back to its former glory. I hope you know how special you are, Thea-Driel, to the kingdom...to me," he whispered, kissing me gently.

The love I felt for him swept through me as I buried my face in the crook of his neck. Reaching up, I sneaked my hands under his tunic and gently brushed over his well-defined stomach as it tensed in response to my touch. Seeing the look of desire in his eyes, I didn't have to wait long before he crushed my lips to his while his fingers in turn caressed my skin, slowly moving up towards my breasts. He then lay back against the hard ground and pulled me on top of him so I straddled him. Slowly his hands lowered, caressing the inside of my thigh in a circular motion, as I began to throb at his intimate touch, wanting more. It was then that I let go, letting instinct take over as our hands explored each other's bodies.

A little while later, we stopped before we reached the point of no return, and lay there, letting our breathing slow down. Yes...he had certainly managed to distract me from tomorrow, I thought to myself.

SEVENTEEN

THE WINTER SOLSTICE BALL...OH, AND THE LITTLE MATTER OF MY CORONATION

"Time to get up!" Eli sang cheerily as he opened my bedroom door. Groaning, I threw my pillow over my head, trying desperately to use my magic to make myself invisible.

"Thea, you look terrible!" he said unhelpfully, kicking the end of my bed. I guessed I didn't have invisibility then.

"You can't hide," he scolded in delight. "Get up! You have so much to do today; Talawen wants to run through your speech one more time, the other guards and I are going to run through your security and you have hair and makeup to do, which, knowing you, will take a while!" he snorted. I threw a pillow at him. "And finally you have to GET DRESSED!" he yelled, grabbing hold of my ankles, trying to pull me from the bed.

Just then, there was another knock at the door followed this time by Inwen's nagging tone. "Thea? Are you in there? You need to get up! You have so much to do," she started to say, walking into my room.

"Is there no such thing as privacy?" I grumbled, forcing myself to sit up. Seeing the smirk Eli gave Inwen, I knew they were just going to pester me until I got up.

"Well, I come bearing food!" Inwen said, trying to entice me with a tray full of breads, pastries and fruit that she placed on my bedside table.

"Do you really expect me to eat all that?" I snarked at her. Clearly I was going to be Miss Attitude today.

"No…but you need to eat something," she replied patiently, as I caught the eye roll she gave Eli. "You have a long day ahead of you and if you haven't already worked it out, it starts now. Come on, shower time," she commanded, pulling on my hand until I reluctantly stood up. "Eli, you need to leave."

"Alright." He grinned. "But if you need any help in the shower, I'm all yours!" he said, waggling his eyebrows suggestively at me. The withering look I shot him was my only response as I continued muttering, heading into the shower before Inwen closed the door behind me.

Twenty minutes later I at least felt awake. Looking in the mirror I took a moment to myself as I thought about the day and its significance. I can do this, I thought, walking determinedly out of the bathroom.

I was really grateful for Inwen's help and reassurances throughout the morning. Eli was good as well, and hardly left my side, explaining that Isaac and the other guards were about, securing the palace and surrounding area. I knew the considerable effort he was making, trying his hardest to act normal, even though the dark circles under his eyes told another story; he was still really worried about Kayla, especially as there had been no news about her whereabouts.

Everywhere was a hive of activity as people rushed from one place to another, carrying all sorts of paraphernalia that was needed for today. I tried to block out the commotion as the three of us went to meet Talawen who, satisfied with the practice run-through of my speech, gave me a quick fatherly hug before releasing me to go and meet the Thills.

Seeing Isaac standing there giving instructions to another guard, I couldn't help but think how handsome he looked already dressed in his formal Thill attire. Looking even more polished than he normally did, his tunic had the elemental emblem emblazoned in silver across the front panel. I could tell he had also tried to tame his hair, but without success as his bangs continued to fall stubbornly into his eyes. As he finished his conversation with the guard, he looked up and saw me staring at him. Smiling, he started to walk over, giving me a smouldering look that instantly began to settle me.

"Hey," he said huskily as he pulled me into a tight embrace.

"Hey right back at you," I replied, snuggling my face into the crook of his neck before kissing him. Taking a deep breath, I enjoyed this intimate moment, even with the hundreds of Elves who were milling around us.

"Let's talk safety," he said, pulling back as he

switched from boyfriend to guard mode. Keeping a hold of my hand he walked me over to a rather intimidating group of Thills, most of whom I now knew personally. Grinning at Janin, Taro and Caleb in particular, I then turned expectantly to Isaac as he began the meeting.

"Thea-Driel's safety is of the highest priority today. There are so many threats out there, Elves as well as other races that would prefer her dead so Minen can keep his claim on the throne for good," he started with an air of authority. Even though he didn't say it directly, we all realised Minen would more than likely be behind any attack I'd face.

"You have all been given your assignments and should only leave your position if I authorise it, or you see Thea's life is in immediate danger," he continued, as the Thills all nodded solemnly. Trying not to focus on the fact that 'in immediate danger' could mean I was about to die, I swallowed down the bile that was threatening to make an appearance.

"Thea, the six guards who will be with you throughout the day haven't changed. It's still Janin, Taro, Caleb, Dranid, Eli and I."

Pleased with his choice, I smiled at them a little nervously, trying not to show how I was truly feeling. This was such a big deal.

Dranid looked slightly older than the others and, out of the six of them, was the guard I knew the least about. Like the others though, his posture, standing with his arms pulled back behind him and feet slightly apart, oozed a 'don't mess with me', kick-ass vibe. His dark brown hair hung to just below his shoulders, and as I continued to blatantly stare, now focusing on his face, I realised his hazel eyes were watching me, appraisingly. He gave me a quick smile before turning back to Isaac.

"The six of us won't be leaving you or Inwen alone at all today I'm afraid," he announced, thinking this would bother me, but as I turned to Inwen, I could see that, safety aside, she would have no problem appreciating their male forms just as much as me.

"Dismissed," he said as the Thills placed a fist over their hearts and bowed to me.

"To serve and protect," they said in unison. I had another 'wow' moment as I saw clearly how important I was to them.

As the majority of the guards left, my key six came forward to have a separate conversation with Inwen and me.

"We will all be wearing ear pieces and will therefore be able to contact each other at any time. While you and Inwen won't be wearing one, you need to make sure you have this on you at all times," he said, handing me a small silver brooch. "It has a tracking device in it...just in case," he explained, hurrying through the last part as he saw my panicked expression.

"You won't need it, it's just there for protection, we're not going to let anything happen to you," Isaac insisted, holding on to my upper arms as he gazed into my eyes. He spoke in the same calm, authoritative voice he had just used, trying to reassure me.

"You can also activate the brooch yourself by pressing this part," he continued, pointing at the middle part where the sapphire was. "If you find yourself in trouble and need one of us, just press it and we'll come straight away."

Taking a deep breath Inwen and I repeated the

security precautions to them so they knew we understood what to do in different scenarios, and leaving Isaac to discuss a matter with Talawen, Eli walked Inwen and me over to get ready. He was clearly trying to lighten the mood again.

"Only three hours to go ladies, are you sure that's enough time to look beautiful?" he smirked at us. Inwen tried to hit him whilst I stuck out my tongue. Who said a future queen couldn't be juvenile?

"I'll catch up with you later," he confirmed as we stood outside my bedroom. Nalis had promised to help us get ready, which meant she would already be in my room with an additional team who'd be doing our hair and makeup. I clutched the brooch Isaac had given me as we walked into the room.

Starting with our makeup, they plucked, creamed and powdered our faces until they were satisfied. Not letting us have a look, we were then whisked over to another area of my room where hair stylists twisted and plaited sections of our hair into elaborate styles. The final stage was helping us into our dresses, and when they had finished, I was once again led carefully over to stand in front of the mirror ready for the big unveiling. Hearing Inwen's shallow breaths next to me, I knew she was feeling just as nervous as I was.

Looking in the mirror, I let out a small gasp: I hardly recognised myself. I looked radiant! My hair had been done in an elaborate updo with intricate weaving that had been pinned into place with tiny crystals, and my makeup complemented my natural skin tone while emphasising my blue eyes. The overall effect with the dress was simply stunning and made me feel that, if nothing else, I could at least look like a queen! Inwen was just as in awe of her outfit as I was with mine. Unlike my hair, the majority of hers hung down in long curls.

We squealed at each other whilst at the same time trying our hardest not to move and ruin their hard work, and after thanking them profusely I realised this was it, it was time. For the purposes of self-preservation, I withdrew into myself, zoning out from all the outside noises as in a blur I was taken along various corridors, down some stairs and outside where the sun was shining brightly. Standing in position to the side of the main stage, Inwen could see I had entered 'the zone' and left me to it as she answered various questions on my behalf.

After a few minutes or so, warm breath blew around my neck before I was gently kissed. Turning around, I saw it was Isaac standing there, as sexy as ever. Breathing in his delicious scent, he leaned in again, this time to kiss me on my forehead. Behind him I could see my five other personal guards looking on at my appearance with pride.

Eli also took that moment to step forward and leaned in, giving me a kiss on the cheek. "You look beautiful," he whispered, before squeezing my hand, wishing me good luck. Looking tentatively at Isaac I could see he was trying hard not to react to Eli's words, and was pleased when Talawen decided at that moment to come up and address us; his timing really was uncanny.

"They're ready," he said, as I walked numbly up the steps and onto the main staging area, my guards following closely behind.

Stepping out from a partition my breath caught as I looked out on to a sea of faces. There had to be at least a couple of thousand Elves, amongst other races, sitting in the audience, all waiting to hear what I had to say. A hush settled over the congregation as in unison they rose respectfully as I made my way over to the middle of the stage. Before starting, I took a final look at Isaac for reassurance before speaking.

"Elves of our great nation, honoured guests, today is a momentous day as I become queen of our beloved kingdom."

I stopped.

Looking down at the words I had rehearsed, they had now become a blur as I thought about all that had recently happened, not just to me, but all the families out there in the crowd who had lost loved ones due to Minen and his tyrannical ways, as well as those whose family members were still missing...Kayla. I realised at that moment they didn't want to hear their future queen give the politically correct speech Talawen had helped me put together. They wanted a speech that would come from the heart. That recognised their needs and the needs of the whole kingdom. Taking a deep breath, I continued, folding up the now useless script in front of me.

"Since coming back to Aroben, I have seen a nation filled with Elves who know what it means to be part of this great kingdom. Yet we have all suffered hardships and continue to do so. Some of you are wondering where your loved ones are. Have they disappeared? Are they coming back? Others of you have been made to feel like second class citizens, defined purely by the element you wield. I am here today to tell you that as your queen I will end this now.

"We need to create a society that embraces all members for who they are and their unique gifts, and we can only do that if we see ourselves as equal, working together for the same common goal. Like my father and mother, I will give my life to serving you, doing everything in my power to right the wrongs that have been done.

"Today at my coronation, I ask that you pledge your life to me, join with me, and embrace with me what I hold most dear: a future for all. Your loyalty and affection, I will carry forward from this day."

As I finished with the oath of Aneyiln, I held my breath, unsure what the response would be to my unorthodox speech. I didn't have to wait long before I was met with rapturous applause. Elves all around me had risen off their chairs, cheering and clapping at my speech. Turning on shaky legs, I watched as Minen walked towards me holding the royal crown in his outstretched hands. As he placed it on my head, I looked up at him defiantly, not at all surprised to be greeted with a look of burning hatred. Even so, it took all my resolve not to step backwards. Standing still, I raised my chin up at him and smiled, the look of triumph shining on my face as the congregation once again cheered.

Pleased that the speech part of the day I was dreading the most was finally over, I walked in procession towards the Great Hall as the next part of the celebrations, the Winter Solstice Ball, was about to begin. On the way I was met by many well-wishers under the watchful eye of my team, and Inwen was also an ever-welcoming presence behind me, holding onto my train.

The Great Hall looked spectacular, especially with the sun setting in the background. There were hundreds of tables laid out, each with striking blue flowers as the centrepiece. The dignitaries and other

Elves who had been invited for the banquet were already seated, until they stood as one as I entered, all in respectful silence.

With their heads bowed, I made my way up the centre aisle and took my place at the head table with Minen to my right and Talawen my left. On my table were the other four Council Elders, all looking regal in their finery. Talawen explained this would show those present the unity between the throne and Council. My protection team took up position along the wall behind me.

Inwen, who was seated at a table nearby, gave me the thumbs up as we started to eat. Grinning back at her, I knew her gesture was intended to congratulate me on the fact that my coronation had gone without a hitch, and seeing someone waving frantically next to her, I realised it was Bay, looking completely dapper in a black tunic and trousers. I waved back, pleased he could keep Inwen company. Looking around the rest of the room, I saw guards lined up every few feet or so around the periphery of the hall, and knowing Isaac literally had my back, I began to relax.

Completely ignoring Minen on my right, I spent most of the meal in conversation with Talawen. The food was exquisite, consisting of various Elven delicacies I hadn't tried before; however, I laughed out loud in surprise when one of the things on my plate was French fries! Looking round at Eli, knowing this kind gesture had to come from him, I mouthed 'thank you', as I shook my head in disbelief while he tried to look a picture of innocence. He knew I had been hankering for fries since I'd left the human realm.

"That was a very bold move," Talawen commented when Minen was deep in conversation with Elder

Lhinanor. Knowing he was referring to my speech, I grinned back at him. "And," he continued, "I wouldn't have expected anything less. Your parents would have been so proud of you," he finished, smiling warmly at me. Feeling my throat tighten at his kind words, I gave him a watery smile as he squeezed my hand.

When the meal was finally over we went outside into the extensive grounds to give the staff time to clear away the tables and create enough space for dancing. I decided this would be a perfect time to take a bathroom break, and yes, it was very difficult to go when followed by an entourage such as mine. Isaac had warned me that he would be remaining in guard mode throughout the night, which I understood, but even so I sneaked a quick kiss from him before going back outside.

As soon as I was spotted, I was greeted by Elves and other dignitaries wanting to talk to me about various matters, or just to congratulate me on my speech, which I tried to take in my stride. Luckily, after about half an hour of smiling and making light conversation, I was rescued by Talawen who wanted me to meet some friends of his. Realising they weren't of this realm, I tried to work out what species they were. I was positive the first acquaintance was a nymph, due to her ethereal beauty. She held herself poised and graceful, and, with eyes that shone a brilliant turquoise and white flowing hair, you couldn't help but stare at first. The magic surrounding her was certainly strong, coming off her in waves and making her appear to shimmer every now and then.

"Thea, this is Synda, Queen of the Nymphs. She was a good friend and ally of your parents."

Smiling shyly at her, I was secretly impressed I had

correctly guessed her race. I recalled what Isaac had explained previously, that although they had their own kingdom, many preferred to live with other races in their realms and were therefore perfect observers as to what was going on. They could forewarn us of any unusual activity, and remembering that made me appreciate how useful an ally they really were.

"It's an honour to finally meet you, Thea-Driel. Talawen has been singing your praises since your return; we are expecting great things from you," she said kindly, holding out her hand in greeting. Taking it, I was surprised at how cold her touch was, and shivered unexpectedly.

"It's an honour to meet you too. Is your realm near to ours?"

"Not too far, Maesdra is a nine-day journey from here."

Looking back at Talawen, I waited for him to introduce the other friend I was to meet. This creature was in stark contrast to Synda. Standing slightly apart from us, he was short by anyone's standards, around three foot six at the most. He had a look of disinterest plastered all over his face, and his eyes, which were as black as charcoal, seemed to pierce into me, adding to the unfriendly demeanour he was projecting.

"This is Raegog, from the Dwarf realm. He is one of the royal advisors to their king, Graenar. Unfortunately, the king has been unable to join us due to ill health, but we are very pleased to be able to welcome Raegog to the celebrations instead," he exclaimed joyfully, grasping him warmly by the shoulder.

I bit my cheek to stop the laughter threatening to bubble up, as it looked like Raegog would prefer to be anywhere other than here and clearly he didn't like to be touched.

"An honour," he said in a grave voice, bowing his head slightly.

At that moment, trumpets sounded, signalling the start of the ball, which was perfect timing as I wasn't sure what to say to this peculiar Dwarf. The crowd parted, waiting for me to go in first. Making sure Inwen was ready, we walked up the steps and entered the Great Hall, which had been transformed into an elaborate dance floor with seating and a few tables located around the outside.

Annoyingly, the first dance had to be with Minen, but it only lasted a few minutes, both of us desperate for it to end. It was then tradition that any guests present could request the pleasure of a dance, something Isaac had been far from happy about, from both the safety and jealous boyfriend points of view.

My first eager recipient looked part Troll and smelt like one too. Giving Inwen a look of mock terror, I watched as both she and Eli snorted in laughter at my predicament. Fortunately my partner was unaware of what they were doing and instead grabbed hold of my hands, pulling me in close enough that I could touch the sweat running down his face. Yuck, especially as on closer inspection I saw there was something else gross oozing from his face.

By the time my fifth dance was over I was ready for a break, and turned to walk back to Inwen when Callon stood in front of me expectantly. I was surprised he wanted a dance and my heartbeat picked up as I wondered if he had an ulterior motive, the conversation with his father playing in the back of my mind.

Panicking slightly, I tried to reason with the part of my brain that was going into overdrive and worked hard to fix a normal expression on my face. Glancing round I was relieved to see Bay watching us with interest nearby, but as Callon hadn't done anything to me, all Bay could do was shrug helplessly. Trying to focus on dancing, I held my arms out as he gripped on to me awkwardly, his hands clammy and sweaty. Perspiration gathering on his forehead, he refused to look me in the eyes.

"What did you think of my speech?" I asked, my snippiness coming back with a vengeance as we moved around the dance floor. If he was going to start something, I was prepared and wasn't going to pretend I didn't know he was up to something.

Everyone around us was enjoying the music and by this point many couples had ventured onto the dance floor.

"It was…err…" Callon started, looking around him nervously. I was just about to confront him on why he was being so weird when it happened, and by 'it' I mean complete chaos.

EIGHTEEN

HELL AND CHAOS ALL ROLLED INTO ONE

The first sign that something was wrong was the almighty crash I heard, followed by glass breaking as all sixteen windows shattered in front of us. Everyone began screaming as they tried to run for cover whilst shards of glass rained down on us. However frozen I was to the spot, my mouth gaped open in horror as two huge dragons then proceeded to claw their way through the now wide open spaces where the windows had once been. They were enormous beasts, very similar in shape and size to the illustrations I had seen back in the human world. Both were at least ten feet tall and their reptilian bodies were covered in scales that were a deep blue in colour, almost black. Their tails looked incredibly powerful as they swept them back and forth, easily knocking over Elves and other

Faey alike, many of whom fell to their death. Their eyes were a striking red and flashed in anger as they continued to cause destruction around them, releasing their fiery breath. Guests started screaming, becoming even more frantic as it was increasingly evident there was nowhere to hide. It was then the screams began to take on a whole new meaning as many were now being burnt from the intensity of the flames.

Waking up from the nightmare trance I had entered, I realised how deafening the noise actually was. I didn't notice the building pressure on my arm as Callon gripped it fiercely, digging his nails in and drawing blood as he tried to drag me towards the hall doors. Not sure if he was trying to help keep me safe, or was hurting me because he was petrified, I started to follow at first but then realised we were heading straight towards his father. Elder Lhinanor stood in front of sinister-looking Elves completely covered in black, as well as groups of Trolls and Goblins, many of whom were getting caught up in the carnage around them, killing innocent Faey with sheer delight plastered on their faces. Crap, crap, crap! I thought to myself. Where the hell were Isaac and Eli?

My heart then stopped, fear taking hold as I turned to see that none of them were able to come and help me as all the guards, including my immediate six, were engaged in their own battles. It was only small consolation that they seemed to be holding their own. Refusing to become a victim and meet the same end as my parents, I started struggling against Callon's vice-like grip.

"Let me go!" I yelled at him, as he twisted my arm backwards, causing pain to shoot up into my shoulder. "What the hell are you doing?"

"Finally, something I can be proud of," Lhinanor sneered at him in response, as I was pushed back into his waiting hands. Lhinanor then proceeded to pass me over to a Troll that had to be at least twice my size.

"Double crap," I groaned, realising it was now nearly impossible for me to escape.

At that moment, over the constant cries and screams, I turned as Isaac called out to me.

"Thea!" he shouted as he sliced his sword through his attacker's stomach, killing him instantly. He ran towards me with Eli in tow, as he just managed to duck out of the way of one of the dragon.

The sounds of the carnage continued as another round of fighting broke out when more soldiers – including the Thanes – arrived on scene. The heat was now becoming unbearable and I desperately hoped my friends, who I had come to see as my family, were still safe, having no idea where they were.

Many of the Thills had now realised the situation I was in and had managed to re-group, trying to break through the ring of attackers holding me hostage. I struggled again, trying to break free from the Troll holding me, and by fluke kicked out just at the right moment as Eli's sword pierced through its arm. It howled, dropping me to the ground as it then began to roar with a voice like thunder. Knowing I was seconds from escaping, he lunged at me at the same time as I threw myself backwards, out of his reach and into Isaac's waiting arms.

"Thank the goddess you're alright!" Isaac exclaimed in relief as I clung on to him for dear life. I couldn't stop shaking. Knowing this battle was about me and that I'd almost been captured was too much. It was made worse knowing hundreds of innocent beings, of all races, were now being slaughtered, and the danger was still far from passed.

"Hey, it's okay. Hey, breathe Thea, breathe!" Isaac said soothingly, trying to calm me. I worked on regaining control, knowing I wasn't helping anyone being like this. I could break down later, if I was still alive.

Many of Minen's guards were now barricading the doors, which was now the only possible escape route as the dragons were making it impossible to leave through any of the windows they watched over.

Shouting out orders to the other Thills, Isaac had now positioned me so that I was cocooned in the middle, with Janin and Taro either side of me and Eli standing behind.

"Where are Inwen and Bay?" I shouted whilst Goblins and Trolls everywhere beat their chests, in recognition that they were winning the battle.

"We're here," Bay panted as he came up beside me, dragging Inwen with him. She leaned over in obvious pain. Trying to get closer to her to see what was wrong, I went to move Taro out of my way.

"I've got to help her, let me go!" I shouted hysterically as he grabbed hold of me, pulling me into his chest.

"No! You are our priority Thea, we have to get you to safety," Isaac replied, trying to get me to see reason.

"She got stabbed but she'll be okay, I promise," Bay said with a determined look on his face as he tried to reassure me. He could see I was getting beyond reason. A choked sob came out of me and my breathing began to get shallower by the minute. Feeling like I was going to pass out, I started to give up. This was pointless, there was no escape. I had already lost my parents, who else in my new family was going to die? I thought bleakly.

"I have an idea!" Janin called out seconds later. "Thea, use your magic to blind those by the door! Quick, do it now!" he yelled urgently.

"I can't." I panicked. There had to be at least twenty of them and I had only ever managed it with two. I had also been way calmer then than I was now.

"You can Thea. We've got no other choice!" Eli urged, as he ran forward to fight the Troll that was heading straight for us. Trying to pull myself together, I took a few deep breaths and used the death and destruction around me to fuel my anger and, in turn, my magic. I started by closing my eyes, and pictured those holding us prisoner, focusing in on their faces, imagining they were in complete darkness.

"It's working," Isaac whispered in my ear as one by one Goblins and Trolls alike were shouting out in horror at their temporary blindness.

Using this much energy was exhausting, but I wasn't going to give up, even when I began to sway on the spot. Isaac continued to hold on to me. Slightly disoriented, we suddenly ran forward, determined to escape. Others swarmed to the doors as well, seeing there was now a possibility of freedom. We were almost there when an immense force snatched me out of Isaac's arms and pulled me backwards. Smacking my head on the floor, I groaned as black spots flashed in my periphery. Gingerly I felt a spot on my head and could already feel a huge, egg-shaped bump.

As I continued to be pulled away from the others, through all the debris and dead bodies on the floor, I knew I had a problem as I couldn't see who or what was in control of me.

The Thills tried to run towards me and help but then ended up having to face their own problems as Minen's guards formed a barrier between them and me, starting to attack, many using magic. I could only watch on in horror as this precious gift from our goddess was being used in such a frightening and evil way.

Still looking around for the source of my imprisonment, and stuck in the middle of the hall unable to move, I realised Lhinanor was my captor as he stared at me intently, arms out. Thankfully though, the pressure suddenly disappeared as he was attacked by a Thane. Standing up, I tried to work out whom to go help first.

Isaac and Eli were fighting back to back, surrounded by four Elves, their swords drawn; it was becoming increasingly apparent their fight was too close to call. Then looking to my right I saw Taro and Caleb were standing further apart, both battling a couple of Goblins who were shooting blasts of their element at them and succeeding in pushing them closer and closer to the windows and the waiting dragons.

One of the dragons must have been injured, as part of his tail had been cut off and dark, red blood was oozing out. I expected that this injury might slow it down, but it seemed to fuel him on as he continued to wreak havoc with renewed energy, smashing some nearby tables as well as causing the drapes to catch on fire. Zeroing in on our group, it let out a piercing screech as nearby I saw Janin had begun wielding water at it in three short consecutive bursts.

NINETEEN

A LIFE LOST

Looking back on what happened next, it seemed so surreal, like it happened in slow motion. Backed into a corner, the dragon suddenly charged at Janin who, without any time to react, was picked up in his huge jaws and I watched in horror as he was shaken about like a rag doll.

"No!" I screamed, running towards him, trying to somehow help.

"No! Help! Someone help!" I screamed again, my voice breaking. "Janin, oh my goddess, Janin!"

His tortured screams penetrated deep into my being as Taro and Isaac came up behind me, trying to pull me back into their arms.

"No!" I whispered brokenly. "Janin."

Sobbing, I watched as both Eli and Dranid rushed past us and took on the dragon, Eli shooting arrow upon arrow until they pierced both its eyes, blinding it, whilst Dranid rushed forward and thrust his sword through its armoured scales and into its belly, managing to kill it quickly. Janin's body hung limply in the beast's jaws. As the dragon slumped to the floor I realised what was wrong. Janin wasn't moving. Oh goddess, was he even breathing?

Struggling free, I ran over, falling onto the wooden floor next to him, and as I grabbed a hold of him by the shoulders to see if there was anything I could do, I saw it was too late.

He was already dead.

The anger that began to build in me was all-consuming as I staggered up, looking around but not actually taking anything in. Without realising what I was doing, I let my magic pull on the elements around me. Not just the earth, but energy from the water, air, fire and spirit coursed up through my body. The power that surged was too much and too painful, but I didn't care, nothing mattered anymore as I still held on to all my anger. As a torturous scream came from me, the Great Hall began to shake, causing still-standing tables to fall and many of the chandeliers to come crashing to the ground. A crack appeared in the middle of the floor, running its entire length. It wasn't until the roof started caving in that I heard someone trying to tell me something.

"Thea, stop! It's okay, it's going to be okay." Struggling to keep a hold of all my power, I turned towards the voice to see Isaac standing there with Inwen just behind. I couldn't comprehend what they were saying and just watched as he held out his arms cautiously, unsure as to how I would react, almost like I was a wild animal.

Feeling utterly exhausted, I slumped to the floor just before Isaac pulled me up onto his lap.

"He's dead, it's never going to be okay," I whispered, feeling completely broken, like an empty vessel with nothing more to give.

In contrast to the earlier noise there was now a deathly silence as I realised the battle was over because of me, many of Minen's horde having been instantly killed by the roof collapsing. Those who were still alive had obviously fled.

Somehow we had won, but at what cost? Feeling completely numb, I watched as Isaac gave orders to the Thills and remaining dignitaries standing nearby. With some sense of relief, I saw Talawen had come through this alive.

Inwen held my hand whilst Isaac issued orders. We both sobbed in so much physical and emotional pain, I didn't even notice as Dranid began guiding us towards the hall doors. Thinking Isaac had asked him to take us somewhere I let it happen, and after a while we began to move more quickly, with a sense of urgency that wasn't needed. He took us down a corridor and out to the other side of the palace before I bothered to question him.

"Where are you taking us?" I mumbled, confused, whilst Inwen struggled to keep up with the demanding pace. The stab wound she had received to her stomach was still seeping through her dress in a steady flow and her face was pale due to all the blood loss. We hadn't yet managed to get her a healer.

By this point Dranid had managed to lead us outside into the grounds and we were now heading towards the lake.

"This way...come on," he ordered, pulling harder on my arm as he ignored my question.

Something didn't feel right and I yanked my arm back, coming to a stop.

"No. Where are you taking us?" I said again, feeling more and more like this was a trap. There was no way Isaac would want me to leave him now after what had just happened. Even in all her pain, Inwen was getting increasingly anxious with this strange turn of events.

"Hurry up!" he then snapped angrily, shoving me forward, as all pretence of being my guard, my protector, were forgotten. I stumbled, scraping my hands on the gravel as I fell to the ground. Dranid, becoming exasperated, picked me up and threw me over his shoulder. He then proceeded to walk quickly down the path, dragging an exhausted Inwen next to him.

It was getting really dark now and must have been about one in the morning. I couldn't see clearly, but knew we were getting near our destination as Dranid began to slow down. Struggling to be released, I yelped in pain as he yanked down on my arms to keep me still.

"Now now, Dranid, we don't want to injure the queen too much, do we?" a smug voice spoke from the darkness. Although I couldn't see him, I recognised the voice instantly.

"Minen," I bit out angrily.

As Dranid put me down, I turned to see him standing next to Lhinanor. Callon was nearby, looking terrified as the horror of my kidnapping and his part in it were obviously sinking in. A couple of Goblins who were also standing in the small gathering hissed at me in disgust, but I refused to be intimidated.

Looking back at Minen, I couldn't believe he had succeeded, and was furious. Not just because by capturing and killing me he would be able to seize control over Aroben again, which was exactly what I had been fighting against, but also because he had taken Inwen prisoner as well and I didn't think it likely she would come out of this alive. I sent a quick prayer to the goddess for help.

"So, Minen," I sneered. "You have me, so let Inwen go. She doesn't mean anything to you," I said, holding my breath to see if it would work.

"On the contrary Thea, we have great plans for Inwen," he said, as the Goblins took a threatening step towards her. Moving in front of her I tried to protect her, which was becoming increasingly difficult as she had become even paler and was now having trouble standing.

"Oh how noble," Minen mocked. "The queen is trying to rescue one of her loyal subjects."

Searching deep within for some sort of hidden strength I raised my chin, trying to look nonchalant. "You can't expect to get away with this. My guards will already be searching for us, and when caught you'll be tried for all the murders you committed. I'll make you pay for what you've done to this kingdom, and to my parents."

"Thea, Thea, such the drama queen. Surely you don't think I don't know about the tracking device on your broach? Dranid…take it off," he ordered.

I could only look on in desperation as it was ripped off and snapped in half, my back-up plan gone in seconds. Dranid then grabbed hold of my arms, pulling me back against him. The thought of touching him was repulsive as he stank of treachery. I smacked my head back into his and the sickening crunch that followed was immensely satisfying as I realised it must have caused him considerable pain. Feeling completely betrayed by him, I turned and gave him a look of disgust.

"You are supposed to be a Thill guard! How could you betray the others, I…arrgghh," I screamed as he retaliated by kicking me in the knee, the same knee I had hurt back in training. Falling to the floor, the familiar throbbing made me think the kneecap had been smashed again. I curled up, trying to stifle my whimpers.

"Enough of this," Minen shouted. "We've wasted enough time here, let's go."

I yelped as once again Dranid picked me up roughly, holding me in his arms. At least this time it wasn't over the shoulder as I clutched my knee, trying to lessen our movement. After walking for what felt like hours, the pain and dizziness became too much and I slipped into unconsciousness.

TWENTY

THE DARKEST NIGHT

"Thea...Thea, please wake up," a broken voice whispered. I could feel someone nudging my shoulder. "What are we going to do? Thea...you need to help me, I don't want to die here!" the same voice continued, until it broke down sobbing.

Feeling completely disoriented I slowly came to, realising we had stopped moving and were now lying on a cold, damp floor. Opening my eyes I saw Inwen peering down at me anxiously.

"You're awake!" she exclaimed in relief. "I thought you were never going to wake up, you've been unconscious for hours."

Sitting up slowly I tried to get my bearings, which proved difficult as the only light was coming from a dimly lit torch nearby, hanging from a wall.

"What is this place?" I asked. The air felt musty and damp, like we were underground, and a cold chill continued to seep through the gaps of a large wooden door.

"We're in the Blunran Mountains, about a day's walk from the palace. This area is extensively mined for the abundance of jewels that can be found. There are tunnels all through this place."

"Are you okay? Your wound...what happened?" I asked, trying to lie her down so I could have a look.

"I'm alright. It was one of the Goblins...I got stabbed," she said softly before wincing at my touch. The wound looked anything but okay and still hadn't stopped bleeding. Judging by how sluggish her movements were becoming, I didn't give her long before she passed out.

"You'll be fine. I'm sure we'll be rescued soon," I said with false confidence.

Not seeing the way we had entered I had no idea how far from the main entrance we were, or which way we would need to go to escape, and I doubted Inwen would be any help soon. With a feeling of hopelessness overwhelming me, I looked down at my friend in pain. There must be something I can do, I thought, refusing to accept there would be another life lost due to Minen.

Suddenly, inspiration hit me and I sat up in surprise. Of course! Maybe, just maybe, I could use my spirit element to heal her. Yes, I realised this was a near impossible task as I hadn't been trained as a healer, but at least it gave me something to focus on, as well as a glimmer of hope that she would be alright.

Explaining my thinking to Inwen, a glimmer of

hope flashed across her face. If only I could remember what Healer Farwen had done. It wasn't like I hadn't seen him heal me enough recently.

"Think, Thea!" I muttered to myself.

Shifting slightly, I carefully moved my knee, which was still causing me agony, when another thought struck me. Surely if I could heal Inwen, I would be able to heal myself? Inwen first, though, as she was much worse off than me.

Picturing how Farwen had placed his hands on all of my injuries, I did the same on Inwen's stomach. Closing my eyes, I took some deep breaths as my heart thumped wildly in anticipation of what I was going to try to do.

Reaching out for my magic, I enjoyed the feel of it swirling around me, this time a warm and comforting presence. Like I had done earlier in the Great Hall, I also drew magic from the earth and air around me, asking for its help, and immediately felt stronger as the magic began to hum inside me, like it was getting impatient and wanted to be used. Praying again to the goddess for strength, I willed the magic through my palms and onto Inwen's stomach.

Soon I could feel the growing warmth that was building in my hands being transferred to her, and as they began to glow, we both gasped. Next the heat reached an unbearable level and then time seemed to stop. It was only when I felt the magic completely leave my body that I looked down at the wound to see if I had made any difference.

"It worked!" I yelped in surprise, suddenly exhausted. The wound had closed up, leaving behind a faint pink mark, and the colour that was now returning to Inwen's face meant she was clearly beginning to feel better.

"Not even Farwen could completely heal me, so how could I fully heal you?" I thought out loud. "How are you feeling?" I asked, feeling euphoric that I'd managed to save my friend's life.

"Completely normal," she exclaimed, standing up to prove it.

"I've never heard of a healer being able to do that either. They are only supposed to be able to speed the healing process up, that's all. I knew you were special! What do you think you did differently?"

"The only thing I can think of is that I called upon the air and earth elements to help me as well, which Farwen can't do as he's only a Spirit Elf. That makes sense, I suppose," I laughed, completely in awe that the goddess would give me such an amazing gift.

Turning to look at my knee, I lifted the folds of my dress up and repeated the same process. It didn't take as long to work, possibly as my injury wasn't as bad, and I was soon jumping up and down with Inwen, giggling hysterically at the thought that we might survive this.

When we had both calmed down, my thoughts turned to Isaac, Eli and the other Thills, and I wondered what they were doing at this moment. I wished I could be with them and reassure them I was fine, which I was, at least for the moment. They had been through so much. Not only had Inwen and I been kidnapped, they had been betrayed by Dranid, one of their own, and Janin had been killed. I doubted Bay and Logan were faring any better either, knowing how important Inwen was to them.

Picturing Isaac in my head, I imagined the feel of his touch on my skin and the warmth one of his kisses always brought. I was determined to come out of this in one piece; I grinned to myself, thinking of the unfinished business he and I had.

"What's with the goofy look?" Inwen smirked, looking like she already knew.

"Just wondering what Isaac's up to." I blushed, embarrassed by the direction my thoughts had taken me. "I have a feeling all of our boys are probably going mad right now wondering where we are."

"Yup, Bay will be spitting blood, but they'll come rescue us soon, I know it."

"Well in the meantime we need to see how we can help ourselves and find a way to escape."

Taking another look at the cave we were in, I saw a bowl of bread and two flasks of water had been placed on a small rocky ledge. There was no bedding I could see, or blankets. Great, I thought, Minen's plan was obviously for us to freeze to death. In fact, I couldn't understand why he hadn't just killed us already. I was the only thing standing in his way from rightfully being able to rule over Aroben. It just didn't make sense. I was sure he would make everything clear soon enough.

Looking over at the wooden door, I realised it was the only way in and out, and didn't seem to have any lock on it, but after yanking hard I realised it wouldn't budge, guessing it was being kept in place with magic. It had a peephole around head height that was obviously so they could check on us, but it could only be opened from one side.

"Do you think there are any guards outside the door?" I asked.

"Let's find out!" she said with renewed enthusiasm, walking up to the door and kicking it with a force I hadn't believed her capable of.

"Hey," she shouted. "Let us out!"

After a couple of minutes of banging we were just about to give up when a pair of yellow eyes looked through the gap at us. Hissing, the Goblin did little else but stare at us before closing the slat.

"Well that answers that question!" she laughed. "What now?"

Turning to face the door, I put my palms out and tried to use my magic to open it but it still wouldn't budge. Frustrated, I turned to Inwen for further ideas but she just shrugged in response.

"I guess we wait," she said. "It won't be long before Minen comes back, especially if he has plans for us."

It ended up feeling like hours had passed before there was any activity behind our door. Both Inwen and I stood up, taking defensive positions next to each other. Hearing someone mutter what sounded like a spell, the door immediately swung open and Minen walked in with Dranid and one of the Goblins that I recognised as having been there at our kidnapping.

"Lovely accommodation, Minen. A five-star meal and luxury bedding...what more could we want?" I said, sarcasm dripping off me. I backed up slightly, ready for him to retaliate.

"Such a feisty one, just like your mother. I'm glad you're both feeling better, but I have to say I'm a little surprised. When we left you were unconscious and Inwen was almost in the same way. There's no way you should be able to stand up with the way Dranid smashed your knee. Care to explain the miraculous recovery?"

Shit. I'd completely forgotten that Minen had no idea about my spirit ability. If he realised how strong I actually was with my magic, he would see me as a more serious threat and have me guarded more closely. This would obviously make escape more difficult. Racking my brains for something to say, it was Inwen who spoke first.

"We weren't as badly injured as you thought," she said in an authoritative voice, but the deep blush spreading across her face told him she wasn't completely telling the truth.

Without warning, Minen nodded at Dranid who walked towards Inwen with a sour look on his face. Before I had time to react, he pushed his dagger right into her stomach, twisting it viciously to the right before he pulled it back out again. She looked up at me in surprise, her mouth opening to make a silent 'o' before slumping to the floor.

Realising Minen had done this to see if we were lying about how we'd recovered, he obviously thought I was the healer. Even though I knew my secret would soon be revealed, I didn't hesitate before kneeling beside her and performing the ritual I had done earlier that day. Exhausted, I sat back, wiping my brow, and waited anxiously to see if it had worked. After a few minutes she groaned, which was like music to my ears. Looking down at her stomach all that remained of the wound was a faint pink line, just like the other one.

However relieved I was, I was so pissed at Minen I started to tremble and could feel the anger burn through my veins at what he was now putting me through. I made a move towards him before I was yanked back by cold, hard fingers squeezing painfully around my arms.

"Smostak, that's enough," Minen said to the Goblin, as my arms were released. "Thea isn't stupid enough to try anything, are you, Thea?"

Giving him a defiant glare, I stood back, willing my now trembling legs to hold my weight.

"It looks like Talawen has once again been holding out on me," he continued to no one in particular. "You obviously have an affinity to spirit...you are a rare commodity indeed. I'm also guessing you are able to wield the other elements?" he said, looking at me expectantly.

My silence was telling enough and caused the tension to rise to new heights as he reappraised me shrewdly.

"Not going to answer? That's fine, we have ways of making you talk, especially considering how useful you are going to be to our cause," he finished before sweeping out of the room with the others.

"Oh my goddess," I whispered, releasing a breath. I had such a sense of foreboding that the 'cause' he was referring to was the reason why Elves were disappearing. I continued to stare angrily at the back of the now closed door. I couldn't let him see he was getting to me, or let on that I might know what he was up to.

TWENTY-ONE

A NEW BRAND OF TORTURE

It wasn't until the following day that we heard voices again, this time outside our door. Inwen and I gave a look to each other, wondering what was in store for us now. That ominous feeling came back, knowing they obviously wanted us for something to do with our elements.

When the door opened, we were greeted by Dranid and the Goblin Smostak, but no Minen. They pushed us roughly into the corridor after placing metal cuffs linked with a chain around our wrists and ankles. At the slightest movement in the restraints, a sharp tingling pain, like pins and needles but worse, would shoot up my legs and arms, and looking at Inwen and seeing her grimace, I realised she was experiencing a similar pain. I guessed it was the iron mixed in with the metal that was causing us to experience this, knowing that it's like poison to Elves. Already my wrists and ankles had become red raw.

Walking down one dark tunnel into another, I had no idea where we were headed and gave up trying to remember all the turns to help us escape. They each looked the same. Dark, oppressive spaces with torches lit up, hanging from the wall every couple of metres or so. The air still smelt damp and musty out here, just like in our prison, but now there was something else mixed in, creating an aroma that I couldn't quite place. It was almost like the smell of magic in the air gone wrong, but that didn't make sense.

It was then that I heard something that terrified me. The sounds of screams and wails echoed down the corridor, getting louder with each step we took.

"What's that?" Inwen whispered, the panic clearly noticeable in the tremor of her voice.

"I don't know, but I have a feeling we're going to find out," I murmured worriedly in reply.

The sounds of torture continued until we finally made it out into a large dome-shaped room that looked like a junction, as it had at least five tunnels leading off from it in all directions. Taking one of the ones on the right, we eventually entered what looked like a meeting room, as it had a large wooden table taking up most of the space in the middle, with maps and plans covering most of it. In the far corner was a smaller table containing just a single oil lamp that projected an eerie feel to the room. Stepping forward from a hidden alcove, Minen and Lhinanor came over to us.

I scowled at them both, wondering if Lhinanor's son was nearby. Even though Callon had played a part in my capture and the subsequent destruction back at the palace, I had begun to feel sorry for him. Not just because of the way his father treated him, but because of his unwillingness to get involved. I felt sure wherever he was, Callon was beating himself up knowing his silence meant many had needlessly died.

"Ahh, our highness has arrived," Lhinanor jeered at me.

I spat in his face. "Lhinanor...always a pleasure...you worthless piece of —"

"Enough," Minen interrupted, as Lhinanor glared back at me, wiping my saliva from his face.

"It is time, Thea, for you to see what I have been up to," he announced, as Smostak let out a tittering laugh, grinning at me. This obviously wasn't going to be good.

We walked down yet another corridor in single file; Minen and Lhinanor headed up the front whilst four or five guards surrounded Inwen and me as we brought up the rear.

Soon the screams started up again and I willed myself to keep it together, picturing Isaac in my mind to help soothe my already frayed nerves.

I knew we were about to see where the noise was coming from as even the air became heavier and oppressive magic seemed to hum all around us, somehow making everything seem dense. I then froze. The sight greeting me made bile rise up my throat. We were in a room that held rows and rows of cells, all full of Elves in various states of decay. Some turned vacantly to look at us, unable or unwilling to move. It was just like some horror story and was made worse when I realised some of the Elves being held prisoner couldn't have been any older than ten.

Kayla. Goddess, where was she? Was she here? I panicked, looking around to try and see her kind and gentle face amongst the others, but she was nowhere to be seen. Was that a blessing? I wasn't quite sure as I swallowed down bile that was threatening to surface.

The sight that had greeted us and the knowledge that Minen really was responsible for all the kidnappings became too much for us both. Inwen started weeping as I could tell she recognised some of the faces that were staring back at her. I squeezed her hand tighter, not sure what to say. My head was reeling at what I saw before me.

But then somehow, unbelievably, it got worse.

Unable to stop the shaking that had taken hold of my hands, we walked past this living hell into another smaller room that had four tables positioned in the corners. On each one, an Elf had been strapped down, and none of them were moving. It looked like they were either unconscious or had been drugged. Other Elves who looked like healers in their white coats leaned over them, performing some sort of procedure as they were each assisted by a Goblin, and next to each table was a tray containing various metal instruments, some already covered in blood.

I couldn't stop it then: I retched, my body's way of trying to reject what it was seeing. The shaking now took a hold over most of my body as I threw up on the floor in front of me and I tried to stop myself hyperventilating.

Why? Why was he doing this? Oh goddess, please make sure Kayla is alright, I pleaded as another round of retching took over.

"Really Thea-Driel, control yourself," Minen said in exasperation. "This is necessary, as you'll soon see."

I snorted, trying to clear my head of the images I was being subjected to.

"Healer Karmas," Minen called out to a dark-haired female. "Please explain the purpose of your experiments to Thea and her friend."

The excited look on the healer's face completely threw me as she started to speak in an animated tone. I had thought she might have been here under duress.

"We are creating a new breed, a super race if you will, who will have the ability to wield any element as well as having superior strength. First we take an Elf with an affinity to a particular element and then extract it, placing it into one of our volunteers. At first we were unsuccessful in getting the affinity to stay in the host, but we soon realised what the problem was."

The sicker the story became, the higher her voice rose. I couldn't believe what she was saying; this was the stuff of horror movies.

"You see, it soon became apparent our volunteers were too old for the element to be embedded and wielded by them, so we looked for younger volunteers..." she continued as my body went numb. I zoned out from what she was saying for a few moments, unable to process how someone could treat another living being in this way.

"...and it's worked!" she exclaimed delightedly. "The younger the Elf, the easier it is for the elements to affiliate with the host. We aren't as advanced as we hoped to be by now, though, as we have only managed to get an Elf to take on one other element, no more than that, so that's our next step. The other problem we've had is that Spirit Elves are in short supply..." she trailed off as what she had just said began to sink in. Oh no, no, no! This can't be why they want me! Now I understood what Minen had meant when he said I'd be part of the cause. Even Inwen must have realised what the plan was as she began to wail in earnest.

Unconsciously I started to back away until I met resistance. Turning, I saw Smostak grinning down at me as his massive frame blocked my exit.

"No!" I screamed at Minen, as I looked around wildly for another exit. "No...I'm not going to be part of this. You're all mad! Why? Why are you doing this? We don't need a super race! The goddess Elebrin gave each of us different elements so we could work together. There is no need for this...what you are doing...it's sick!" I finished lamely, at a loss as to how I could get Minen to see sense.

"Ahh, that's where you are wrong Thea," Minen spoke up, delighted at the look of torment on my face.

"You see, I realised long ago the flaws of the Elven race. We are weak, many of us useless, solely depending on which element is favoured. That's why we started experimenting on with Elves with an earth affinity. They're useless! No one would miss them," he continued manically, completely lost in his own thoughts. "No, we must become a master race, all powerful, not reliant on each other or another species of Faey. This is the only way and already it's begun! We have just been waiting for the right moment to continue, and here you are!"

"Why are the Goblins helping?" I asked, trying to stall for time. "You yourself have just said it's a master Elf race you are trying to create. What do they get out of it?"

"The Goblins? I would have thought you'd have realised why, Thea. Such a greedy race," he replied gleefully, as Smostak hissed at him. "They were more than willing to help with my cause in return for jewels. The Blunran Mountains are a perfect source of gems ready for them to excavate, and in return they capture any type of Elf we need. It's perfect you see. The mountains are also the ideal location for us to do our experimentations as no one would think to look in the tunnels. They even act as a sound barrier for all the noise our volunteers make," he said, waving dismissively at the now unconscious Elves. I was sure they hadn't always been in the state they were in now.

"Some Goblins such as Smostak here have even volunteered to be a host and to create their own super race. This is something I'm considering, as long as it works to our advantage of course. And not just Goblins, there are so many types of Faey, who knows what might happen?"

Groaning, I bent over as my now empty stomach continued to clench. Minen was completely mad and if he continued, the Faey world would never be the same again.

TWENTY-TWO

BETRAYAL AND DECEPTION
ISAAC

The misery was overwhelming as dark thoughts clutched at my mind. I couldn't believe it, I had failed again. Everything was a mess, and for all I knew Thea could already be dead at the hands of Minen. I should have known it was a trap, as his soldiers and Goblins seemed to back down a little too quickly after Thea made them temporarily blind and most of the hall had collapsed. I should have guessed they were just regrouping elsewhere.

"Where the hell is she?!" Eli demanded, looking just as frantic as I felt. "It's been five minutes now and we still have no idea where she is!" he continued, glancing around in an anxious manner.

"Inwen's missing as well!" Baylin started, running up to me, with Logan close behind. "They must be together, but only the goddess knows where."

"Wait a minute!" I growled at them. I was desperately aware that the longer they were gone, the harder it was going to be to find them. I closed my eyes, pinching my brows together as I tried to come up with a plan. Knowing it was Thea who had gone missing had caused my normal rational self to disappear, and I wanted to go punch something. If Minen had done anything to her – anything at all – I was going to kill him. Hell, I was going to kill him anyway for what he'd already done. Janin's death would be avenged. However, I couldn't think about that right now, there would be time to grieve for his soul later.

Looking around me I whistled loudly, gaining the attention of the Thills nearest me. As they ran up I looked around at the familiar faces and realised someone was missing. Dranid.

"Where's Dranid?" I asked, suspicion sinking in that possibly he had something to do with the girls' disappearance. When no one answered, I asked again and turned to Eli to see if he had any idea, but he just shrugged as once again I was met with silence. I didn't have to wait long before it then dawned on him that Dranid was involved in the girls' abduction, as his face darkened and he cursed loudly.

There was no other explanation for his disappearance, as following Thill protocol he knew he had to report to me straight away when any major incidences occurred. Wondering what on earth he could have done with them and why, Bay interrupted my thoughts, confirming aloud what I already knew.

"He's definitely not here…do you think he's got something to do with this?"

"Yes, he must have," Eli answered, as the other guards roared in outcry. The Thills are known for their loyalty, in fact to many we become their new family when they join. Dranid's actions were considered treason, and not just because he'd kidnapped our queen.

"Thinking about it, I remember now…" Taro started. "I swear I saw him leading Thea and Inwen through the entrance doors whilst we were arresting those Goblins, but I didn't think anything of it as I guessed you had given him orders to take them somewhere safe."

Trying not to groan at the realisation we were now up against a trained solider who would know our every move in this sort of situation, I saw that the position we were in was just getting worse and worse by the minute.

Even more time had passed while we stood discussing these latest events, and I'd had enough. I started by ordering my guards to different locations around the palace in pairs, looking for any clues as to where they could have gone. This left Eli and I, and we started planning a wider scale search as we realised they were probably miles away from here now. We still had no idea where they were heading though. Whilst planning potential routes, Talawen hurried up to us, looking grave.

"I've just heard. What can we do to help?" he asked in earnest, waving behind him at the other Council Elders.

"We think Minen has taken Thea and Inwen far away from here by now, and we have no idea as yet of the direction they were heading, or indeed of Minen's plans for them both," I said, trying to sound calm and in control.

"The other guards and I are going to search the surrounding area on horses. Someone must have seen something, or knew about their plans, so if you could liaise with the Thanes and get them to keep looking here I'd be grateful. I'm guessing you and the other Elders will need to take charge here and deal with the backlash?"

"Yes indeed," Talawen replied sombrely. "We fear that the death toll is going to be in the high hundreds. I can't even imagine what Elves around the kingdom are going to say when they realise Minen and Lhinanor have both betrayed us. I was sorry also to hear from Caro about Dranid. You must find them, so justice can be served, and please...bring our queen and Inwen back unharmed. If something was to happen to them..." he choked before walking off.

With renewed vigour, I rounded up about fifteen of the Thills as well as Baylin and Logan and we set off in two groups; I led one group and Taro led the other.

When we were about five miles north of the palace, even with the surrounding darkness, I could see that someone or something had come through quite recently. The leaves had been trampled by what looked like horses and the smell of the mud on the ground was too much like Goblin to have been a coincidence. They had definitely been this way, I thought, as I charged ahead on foot to see if I could see anyone in the distance. However, after about ten minutes, Eli swore loudly as the scent followed an easterly direction but stopped abruptly as it led us to a river.

"There's no chance of finding them now. They

could be anywhere!" Bay said, bringing up the rear. He had come with us while Logan had gone in Taro's group.

"I know. This is a dead end now. Let's hope Talawen has news for us back at the palace," Eli said as he came up next to me on his horse, Naeri.

Knowing they were right, I sighed. We weren't getting anywhere. Nodding to the other Thills to let them know we were heading back, I got back on Terin and turned him around. Seeing the rising sun meant Thea had been captive for about five hours by now. If there were no leads back at the palace, I wasn't going to hold out much hope of them ever being found.

Arriving back in the courtyard, I had a flashback to a time the week before when I had had a rare moment of peace with Thea. I'd been trying to distract her from all the commotion of the ball's preparations, as I could see the strain it was causing her. Finally, the only way I could get her to completely relax was to tickle her mercilessly, and I smiled at the memory. The only way she got me to stop was by kissing me, and I was quite happy with her bargaining methods.

Earlier that day, I had gone with Thea for her elemental test knowing she would pass with flying colours. Not that I had let on, but her skill with the dagger and sword was superb and she followed a style of fighting very much like her father's. When she had fixed that determined look on her face and gone into fight mode, there was no stopping her, and that was exactly what she was like in the test. I have to say she was also incredibly sexy jumping, twisting and turning as she had, especially when every now and then she'd shot me a grin and her whole face would light up.

I still can't believe she chose me over Eli. I thought

he'd be the winner for sure, due to how long he had known her and the strong relationship they obviously had. Whether she had chosen me or not, I knew I wouldn't give up trying to find her. I owed that to the memory of her parents, if nothing else.

Handing Terin over to a stable hand, I headed inside to look for either Talawen or Renad, the Head Thane. Whilst the Thills' sole focus was the royal family and their safety, the Thanes had a responsibility to protect and defend the general public from all sorts of threats they might face. For that reason they had been very much involved in particular with the disappearances of the Earth Elves.

Walking down the corridor I saw Solan, Renad's second in command pacing back and forth agitatedly.

"Did you find anything?" he asked, looking relieved upon seeing our return.

When I shook my head he continued, "One of our team managed to capture a Goblin who had been seen with Minen at the ball tonight. He's injured, so we're thinking that's why the others left him behind. He hasn't got long left, but might give you some information about the queen's whereabouts. He hasn't said anything to us yet but you might have better luck persuading him," Solan said suggestively, raising his eyebrows. "Renad's holding him in one of the one Council chambers. Hurry!" he insisted.

Taking a small team with me, consisting of Taro, Caleb, Baylin, Logan and Eli, we ran down the corridor into a part of the palace that was fairly deserted, and I could see why.

The screams coming from the chamber room were horrific, but I didn't care, knowing that animal inside had been involved in the terrorist attack tonight as well as possibly knowing where Thea might be being held. The two Thanes outside the door moved to one side as I braced myself for goddess knows what on the other side.

The first thing that greeted me was the overwhelming smell of blood mixed with vomit and rotting flesh. As we had been warned, he clearly didn't have long left. Over in the corner, Renad was standing over a cowering Goblin who I could see was having trouble breathing. His body looked beaten to a pulp, especially his face, which was covered in old, crusted blood as well as wounds that were openly weeping.

Upon my arrival, Renad moved back out of the way and I turned, ordering the others to wait outside. They all, especially Eli, tried to protest at first as they all had a reason to want to seek revenge, but this was my fight and it was personal.

I couldn't seem to put anything into perspective as all I wanted to do was rip his head off, but thankfully Renad was around to stop me killing him before I had the answers I desperately needed. I took slow steps forward. It wasn't common knowledge that I had an affinity to spirit as well as water; I hadn't even shared this with Thea, although Talawen knew. The problem was that using spirit didn't come as naturally to me. However, for this, I would use any means necessary to get the truth from him.

"Where is she?" I growled, my voice sounding hoarser than I expected.

"Where is she?!" I shouted again, not giving him a chance to respond the first time.

The Goblin turned to look up at me as he lay sprawled on the stone floor. He leant on his arms, trying to move as his breathing continued to be raspy and laboured. It sounded like there was blood on his lungs. Finally, mustering up the strength, he started laughing, muttering to himself in his own language.

"The queen is long gone now!" he spat out. "Lord Minen, the true and rightful ruler of this kingdom will soon be victorious, you'll see!" he finished gleefully as another round of coughing ensued.

Positioning myself by his head so I could get a clear look at him, I summoned my strength and harnessed spirit to help me. I could see the look of surprise on his face as he suddenly registered what I was able to do. Ignoring the tortured expression that appeared on his face due to the pain I was inflicting on him with my mind, I increased the pressure, getting him to feel even more misery and torment.

"No!" he screamed. "I'm not going to tell you anything! You won't get me to speak!" he whimpered as he cradled his head.

"Where is she?" I demanded again, looking to Renad to assist.

Stepping forward, Renad moved his hands out in front of him, cupping them together at first as he used his affinity to air to lift the Goblin up. He then pushed them out forcefully, causing the Goblin to slam into the wall, sending a picture of an unknown dignitary falling to the floor. He then dropped to the floor as the screams started again; the Goblin tried once again to move, even though he was too weak to do so. His arm lay awkwardly next to him, clearly broken. With renewed energy, I focused more spirit into him, knowing the moment it finally began to work. As he began writhing and moaning incoherently, I stopped, waiting to see if he would give me the response I desperately needed. The Goblin's breaths were now coming out in short gasps as Renad moved to hold him up against the wall.

"Blunran," he moaned. "Queen Thea-Driel is being held in Blunran Mountains, but you're going to be too late! Minen has great plans for her! It was never about just taking her throne," he sneered, fixing his bloodshot eyes on to me.

"Explain!" Renad snarled, as he tightened his hold around the Goblin's neck. The idea that there was more to this than I had originally thought terrified me and I struggled to keep it together. What the hell was he talking about? The Goblin started sniggering again and I began losing my cool, punching him in the face. I felt like the Goblin knew something else that he still hadn't shared – yet. I had to find out what it was.

As I started a third round of torture, his whole body shook and he shrieked hysterically. "Fine...no more. It won't make any difference anyway. I'll tell you..." He swallowed painfully before continuing. "Lord Minen knows what needs to be done to save your pathetic race. He's building his own supreme race of Elves who will be able to wield any element, not just one. That's why he's been taking all your Earth Elves, to look for ways to extract their ability whilst experimenting on others, trying to get them to harness their ability, like a host. Minen's almost there, and he can certainly use Thea's affinity to fire to help him. When it's the next full moon...he'll almost be finished, he just needs more Spirit Elves, but there's never enough!"

Watching me, he started laughing again as I realised the implications of what he was saying. Oh my goddess! Thea was going to be tortured. My mind reeled at finally uncovering Minen's plan and what he had been up to. I looked at Renad and could see he wasn't faring any better upon hearing this information. I felt so many emotions at once: fear for Thea, Inwen and all the other Elves who were currently held hostage, amazement that one man could be so mad and have so much power. It was overwhelming. Who did Minen think he was? He had caused me and thousands of others so much misery. I had to stop him, and it started now, I thought as I sliced the Goblin's head clean off with my sword. Without turning back, I walked out of the room and could hear Renad following.

Right outside, the others were waiting. Eli came straight up, looking at me expectantly with Baylin just behind. Eli knew me well enough by now to read from my expression that I'd heard what I wanted to hear and that it wasn't good news.

"They're at Blunran Mountains," I started, watching the look of relief appear on their faces that we knew their location. "They're all there...all the Earth Elves as well, Kayla included," I said turning to face Eli. I knew this was where she was being kept, I just didn't know if we were too late, for any of them.

Taking a breath, I continued. "Minen's got them all...the Goblin confirmed it. He's experimenting on them to build a super race. He's mad, he wants all Elves to be able to wield all the elements, like we're not strong enough as we are. He took Thea, not just because she has now become queen and has therefore taken the throne away from him: he's also taken her hostage so her elements can be extracted out of her. They're going to torture her," I choked, looking desperately at Eli. "I'm just hoping upon hope he doesn't know she can wield spirit. Seeing as there aren't many Spirit Elves, if he finds out, she won't survive this..."

I didn't need to finish as the others realised what I was getting at. Poor Baylin had gone completely pale, the anguish clearly showing on his face. Not only was he obviously distressed about Thea, but you could see he knew Inwen was going to meet a similar fate, unless we did something about it.

"Renad, get the Thanes together and meet me in the Council chambers, we need to plan what to do next." He nodded at me before leaving. Although the Thanes were their own separate unit of our law enforcement, as Head Thill, and because this was a matter involving our queen, I automatically became in charge of both units.

"What? Why aren't we going now? Come on!" Baylin urged in frustration, Logan nodding in agreement.

"We can't rush in there. If we want to get them out alive, we need to plan this. From what the Goblin said we've got until the next full moon before anything else is going to happen. That's when he's going to experiment next."

"That's in eight days' time!"

"I know, it sounds like a long time but I have a plan!" I explained as eyes looked expectantly at me.

"Come on," I commanded, heading towards the chambers.

TWENTY-THREE

IS ANYBODY OUT THERE?

THEA

It had been about a week since Minen's revelation, or so Inwen and I thought, as we couldn't use daylight to give us an indication. We were back in our room in what felt like the middle of nowhere and I wondered how deep underground we were – and, more importantly, how far from rescue.

Just sitting here doing nothing meant our minds were replaying the hideousness of what we had witnessed back in the extraction chambers. The worst part was the waiting game Inwen and I found ourselves in, as we still hadn't worked out a way of escape and knew that what he had planned for us would surely happen at some point soon. The suspense of waiting for the door to open and for one or both of us to be dragged off was unbearable, and so I spent most of my time curled up, hugging my knees to my chest and wishing I was anywhere but there. We still didn't have any clue where Kayla was or if the Elves Inwen had recognised were alive.

I also kept thinking about Isaac. Where was he? Or Eli? Inwen and I were both beginning to lose hope that they would find us. Surely they would have come by now if they had known where we were? Rocking again, the panic continued to bubble away even when I tried to calm down by picturing them both in my head. "He will come, they won't leave us," I whispered to no one in particular.

Looking around me again for the millionth time as though an escape route would magically appear, I sat up, hearing movement outside. Once the door opened, I saw it was Dranid and two Goblins I hadn't seen before.

"You're to come with us," one of them commanded in a gravelly voice.

"Where?" I replied anxiously, realising they were looking at just me, but they refused to answer. Inwen wouldn't be with me this time, and I didn't know if this was a good thing or not. As I got to my feet and backed into the corner furthest away from them, Inwen started shouting.

"You can't take her! Leave her alone!" she shrieked, trying to make her way towards me, but then one of the Goblins grabbed her roughly before she could reach me and smacked her into the wall. I tried to reason with her before she got seriously hurt.

"Inwen, it's okay. I'll be back soon. We'll talk more about our boys when I get back," I said, trying to reassure her whilst secretly knowing this wasn't good.

I didn't bother to resist as once again the cuffs were put around my wrists and ankles and I was led out of the cell. Giving Inwen one last look and what I hoped was a smile of encouragement, the door closed behind me and I could hear her shouts all down the corridor as they led me down the same path as before.

The room with all the prisoners was just as I remembered, and as we walked past the cells, some gave me despairing looks while others had faces filled with pity, like they knew what was going to happen to me. Even Dranid seemed a little more gentle in the way he handled me, which wasn't normal, all of which gave me a sense of foreboding.

There were some prisoners who recognised me, as they bowed in a sign of respect. Some queen I had been, I thought angrily to myself. I was prisoner in this hell hole and couldn't tell anyone what was going on here in the mountains; no one would ever know. Feeling completely frustrated, my head hung down, eyes trailing the dark brown earth as we moved into another tunnelled-out room I hadn't been in before. This one was different to the other ones I had previously been in, but it was pretty obvious it was for 'experimentation purposes', or to call it what it really was, torture. It was pretty empty except for just one single table in the middle with Healer Karmas standing next to it. The irony of what her name as healer was supposed to represent and what she was actually going to do wasn't lost on me.

I jumped as a voice from behind me suddenly filled the room. I hadn't realised there was anyone else in here apart from my guards, and turning, my suspicions as to who it could be were proved correct: Minen. Of course he wouldn't want to miss this, as was further confirmed by the manic grin on his face.

"Thea, how are you my dear? Keeping well I hope?"

I snorted back, giving him a dirty look. As feelings of fear began to overwhelm me, I didn't trust myself to say anything at all at this point.

"It is finally time for you to serve your kingdom and help support our great cause," he started. "Giving us your spirit element will allow us to examine how to share it with others, ready for our super race."

Clearly he was delusional.

"Dranid, if you would, please," he said expectantly, gesturing for me to be placed on the table. Goddess alive, this was it, I thought, sending her a quick prayer. I became frantic, struggling against Dranid's hold, managing to bite down hard on his arm before he swore and released me. Just then one of the other Goblins hit me across the face. That was going to bruise, I thought dazedly, as black spots swam across my vision. Locked into place by a pair of cuffs, I pulled against them, trying desperately to break free, but it was no use. Shooting pains seared up my arms as the magic-infused metal poisoned my skin.

It was all I could do to hold back the tears threatening to appear, and I bit the inside of my cheek to stop from screaming out.

"Our methods aren't as barbaric as you might think, and are highly effective," Minen said calmly, watching the scene in front of him as though it was an everyday occurrence, which it probably was by now.

"We use this machine here, which holds concentrated energy, to pull out the spirit essence from within."

That's when the shaking started. I didn't realise at

first that it was me that was causing it as my body began to shut down, numbing the pain that was about to come. Tears streamed down my face as I was placed on to the table while the machine hovered above me, over my head and chest. Then a humming sound started. It was the strangest thing, knowing something terribly bad was about to happen to me. Knowing that there was nothing I could do to prevent it only made the situation worse, so I let my mind go back to the only place it truly felt safe.

"I love you," I whispered out loud, thinking of Isaac, just as the humming became louder and the pain started.

At first I just had a dull headache, but then quickly it became so much more. It felt like someone was stabbing me repeatedly, and the pain began to spread down my arms and legs, slowly becoming stronger and stronger in intensity until my whole body felt like it was on fire. Terrified this was actually happening, I opened my eyes to check, but was then immediately blinded by the intense light coming from the contraption above. The humming then became high pitched and I cried out in shock, feeling like this moment was never going to end.

"Goddess, please kill me now," I pleaded aloud, as an intense pressure built in my chest.

Screaming, I fought against the invisible force that was trying to extract my element from me.

"No!" I shouted, as suddenly my power surged from me at the same time I heard an explosion. Then everything went blank.

Coming to, I realised I was being carried by two soldiers with Dranid and Smostak up ahead. My head was thumping and I was still so groggy and disoriented after what I had been through. I couldn't believe I'd survived that and wondered if it was only because something had gone wrong. This was further compounded by the fact that although I hurt like hell, I could still feel my magic within me...all of it...including spirit. Relieved and hoping this meant I was still intact, I drifted in and out of consciousness, hearing snippets of conversation about how it had never been seen before. What though? I wasn't sure, but I knew whatever it was Minen wouldn't be happy.

The sobbing was the first thing I noticed, along with the feeling that someone was wiping a wet cloth over my forehead. Opening my eyes, I realised I was back in my cell, and saw Inwen leaning over me with my head in her lap whilst the rest of me lay on the ground.

"You're awake!" she sniffed, leaning down to squeeze me.

I flinched as waves of achiness washed over me. It felt like my whole body had been beaten.

"Oh, sorry." Inwen sniffed again. "Are you okay? I've been so worried. You've been asleep for ages. I didn't think you were going to wake up," she stated, as another round of sobbing started. Sitting up awkwardly, I groaned and clutched my head. It felt like someone was using it to play the drums again.

"I'm okay, I think," I answered cautiously.

Seeing the disbelieving look she gave me, I continued, "No, really...I think I'm fine. It didn't work!" I said, explaining what had happened.

"Are you sure you're okay?" Inwen asked again with a look of disbelief on her face.

"Yes, look!" I insisted, reassuring her by showing her what I could still do. She smiled the moment I sent calming and happy thoughts her way.

"See!"

"Well, why didn't it work?"

"I have no idea, I don't think they've had this problem before, though," I thought out loud, remembering what Dranid had said as I was carried back to the cell

"Goddess, Inwen it was horrible, I felt like I was going to die. I can't go through that again. I thought my soul – my entire being – was torn in half. We have got to think of a way to escape," I added in earnest, as I re-lived the feelings of torture flooding through me. I didn't want to tell her because she didn't need reminding, but I was well aware Inwen hadn't been taken yet, which meant we were under more pressure to leave quickly.

"We will escape," she said simply. "We've got to. The first thing we have to do is work out how to get away from the guards outside our door."

After discussing various alternatives, we came up with a plan. The next time the guards came in to give us food, Inwen would use air to hold them up against the wall, whilst I would make them temporarily blind. Then when they were immobilised, we would leave through the door, trapping them inside as I'd collapse the earth ceiling over the exit.

It was a couple of hours later when our chance came, and I promised Inwen I was well enough to do this even though the achiness hadn't left and exhaustion seemed to be a permanent feature now, as my magic was still so depleted from what I'd just been through.

We tensed, although trying to still appear normal as the door opened and one of our two usual guards walked in with a bowl of unappealing slop and a bucket of water. The other guard was waiting at the door.

"Now!" I shouted as Inwen went into deep concentration and threw both guards at the wall.

"Hurry!" she grunted, the exertion of what she was trying to do showing on her face.

Summoning up my magic, I sent spirit towards them both and watched as they panicked and shouted out in surprise. Realising we didn't have long before someone would hear them, we both ran to the door, and I then pulled my hands in a downwards motion, willing the dirt from the ceiling to collapse. Inwen yelped, stumbling backwards against the tunnel wall as my magic caused a miniature landslide. Impressed with my abilities, I really did feel sometimes I was as powerful as people were telling me.

"Which way now?" I asked, the adrenaline coursing through me at the thought that we were one step closer to freedom.

"Hang on a minute," she replied as she frowned, closing her eyes. Moments later she opened them, giving me a triumphant look. "This way!" she sang happily.

"How do you —?" I started to ask.

"It's my magic!" she interrupted. "I can feel the air from outside, it's calling to me! Come on!"

She started to run down a path when I suddenly called out, "Wait!"

Inwen stopped, turning to look at me in confusion.

"Hurry, we don't have long until they find out what's happened."

"I know, but we need to help the others first. I can't leave knowing they are still trapped and might die while we escape. Even if we do get help, it might be too late. Kayla...we have to get her for Eli, I don't know what will happen to him if she dies," I finished, waiting for her response. I didn't have to wait long.

"You're right," Inwen answered, nodding her head in determination. "We need to go back. It's not like they'll be expecting this, maybe that will work in our favour," she said, thinking about our captors.

Grabbing her hand, we started back down the tunnel the other way towards goddess knows what. I knew we couldn't go the same route the soldiers had taken me the other day, as it had been lined with guards every few feet or so. With this in mind, we started to head down unknown tunnels, knowing if we weren't careful we were more than likely going to get completely lost.

Every step we took, my body tried to resist, knowing we could full well be heading towards our death. Whilst we had both come up with a plan to escape our room, I had no idea how we were going to get the other prisoners out, let alone find Kayla. Still clutching hands, we walked quickly one behind the other as the tunnel we were in began to narrow. Slowing down, we came up to a junction when suddenly the sound of voices came from the turning on our left.

Seeing two soldiers walking towards the very spot where we stood, I turned to Inwen, waving frantically at her, gesturing that we were in trouble. Panicking that we were going to get caught, I then yanked her down next to me, squeezing the life out of her hand and willing them not to see us. Moments later the threat had passed and I looked at Inwen to see she had a similar look as me, relief mixed with astonishment that we had gone unnoticed. Releasing the breath I had been holding, I gave back her now crushed hand, smiling at our good fortune.

It was then that Inwen's smile disappeared and a look of panic replaced the relieved expression that had been there moments before. Looking everywhere around her, she stood up, calling out in a panicked whisper.

"Thea! Thea! Where are you?"

Feeling thoroughly confused I waved my hand in front of her face, not sure what she was playing at.

"What's going on?"

Inwen started to scream before I slapped my hand over her mouth. It was only then, when I called out, that she properly looked in my direction. "Where did you go?!" she hissed in surprise.

"What are you talking about? I've been right here."

"No, you weren't…you disappeared!"

"That's crazy…oh!" I stopped, cutting off what I was about to say. "This is going to sound insane, but I think…maybe…maybe it was me! I was willing us not to be seen. Do you think my spirit magic allowed that to happen?!" I asked Inwen incredulously.

"You're kidding me! I've never heard of anyone being able to do that."

Shutting my eyes to concentrate, I focused once again on disappearing, and hearing Inwen's gasp, I knew it had worked.

"Oh my goddess! You really are something!" she laughed in disbelief.

"Come on!" I said, grabbing hold of her hand and feeling a renewed sense of determination. We could do this.

I don't know what was guiding me, but somehow I knew which way to go. It was like a rope pulling me in a certain direction, and the nearer I got to one particular tunnel, the clearer it became that there was something or someone of importance down there. Slowing our pace, it was Inwen who came to a sudden halt, pulling on my arm in the process.

"Listen!" she whispered, as I too began to hear what sounded like a whimpering coming from behind a door on our right. Seeing it was locked, Inwen and I both used air to pull it open. Peering inside, my heart stopped. It couldn't be...but it was: she was okay! It was Kayla, curled up in a corner with her head in her hands.

"Kayla!" I whispered, swallowing down the sob that was threatening to escape.

"You're alive."

Her dirty, tear-stained face looked up at us both in astonishment and in the next breath she had flung herself at me, holding on tightly as she clung on for dear life.

"You found me! I knew you would! Where's Eli?" she asked all in one big rush. I could feel her trembling as her frail arms continued to squeeze me around the neck.

"He's coming soon, all of them will be coming for us, including Taro!" I said giving her a wink. As she rubbed her face into my neck, I shared a look with Inwen expressing how lucky we had been. But then, maybe it was more than just luck, I thought, thinking of how much love Elebrin had already shown me.

Realising our escape must have been noticed by now, we knew we didn't have much time, so we headed off again down a tunnel that sloped towards another that was just as steep.

It felt like an hour had passed when Inwen began to get excited.

"They're down there!" she exclaimed, pointing to a turning coming up on our right. "Can you hear them?!"

Listening carefully, I could. It had to be the prisoners as every now and then, mixed in with their murmurings, I could hear groaning as well as the humming from that awful machine. Knowing that someone was experiencing the same pain I had, I sped up.

"How are we going to do this?" I asked, looking at Inwen with uncertainty. We had arrived from the other side of the room we had entered before, and observed all the cells that continued to house the Elves trapped inside.

"There's no way I can blind this amount of guards, especially for the length of time it would take us to unlock their doors and free all the prisoners."

Inwen thought for a moment before sharing her plan.

"Kayla waits here," she started, smiling down kindly at her as Kayla's eyes grew wide at the thought of possibly being separated. "You use spirit to 'hide' you and me from everyone. I'll then unlock the doors and whisper to everyone what they need to do when we give them a signal."

"Let's hope they don't start screaming at hearing voices but not being able to see anyone!" I snorted. "I still don't see how we're going to get everyone out. I mean what about all those guards?" I continued worriedly. "It's not like I can make all the captives invisible, there's too many!"

Knowing so many things could go wrong with this plan, the anxiety continued to rise.

"There are twelve guards altogether that I can see. Any Elf prisoners who are able to, will have to help us fight them. If you have any reserves left, you can blind or torment them. It's not the most organised of plans, but it will have to do. There's no other way," Inwen replied.

Nodding in agreement, I found a place for Kayla to hide behind a huge wooden crate, and once again grabbed Inwen's hand. Taking a deep breath we started forward.

TWENTY-FOUR

NO MORE WAITING

ISAAC

"Are we ready yet?!" Eli asked me with growing impatience. I raised my eyebrows in return, knowing he was only speaking to me like this because he was worried about Kayla and Thea, but still. He backed off at my glance. Hopefully it would be enough to remind him who was in charge and that I wasn't to be rushed. Although we both still had feelings for Thea, and even though she had made her decision on whom she wanted to be with, there was still an uneasy tension between the two of us. At least we had agreed to a truce and could focus on what was more important right now: their safety. When Baylin then rushed up and said exactly the same thing Eli had to me, I started to growl.

"Look, I know this wait has been torture – trust me, I feel the same – but there is no way we are going to throw away all this preparation because you're both getting antsy. When the Thanes get here we can go," I finished, turning away from them and walking off towards the other end of the courtyard. I looked down at the plans so the others would think I was busy and not disturb me, but truth be told my nerves were just as frayed as the others' and I was only just keeping them under control.

It had been seven days since we discovered where Thea, Inwen and the other Elves were being held hostage. After lengthy discussions between Renad, Solan, Eli and myself, we decided the only way to actually know their true location in the mountains was to set a trap, with one of our guards being at the centre of it.

By luck Caleb had received word that some of Minen's soldiers were planning to come back into the city to take further Elves tonight, so with this in mind, Solan came up with the idea of getting one of the Thills to go undercover and get captured. This way, due to the extensive underground tunnels at Blunran, we could follow them, hoping he would lead us straight to the hostages...and Minen.

As expected, all the Thills and Thanes volunteered for the job of being captured, including both Solan and Eli, but Renad and I felt it would be better if it was someone more unknown, and definitely someone who had not been at the coronation in case they were recognised. For this reason we went with Eyowel, a youngish Elf who had just joined the Thills. Although he didn't know Thea personally, his commitment to the throne and wanting justice for what had happened meant he was a perfect candidate and completely trustworthy. He had explained to me the other day that his younger brother had been captured just before the coronation, so I knew that, just like me, he had a vested interest and this rescue mission was personal to him as well. We only had an hour to go before we were to lie in wait to see if the enemy would take our bait.

Looking up I saw Talawen walking towards me. He looked exhausted, with worry lines becoming an ever-present feature around his eyes. This past week had taken an immense toll on him and the other Elders. With Aroben in a state of turmoil, and no one to take the throne, Talawen had taken temporary control that was generally received well by the kingdom. Many remembered him from the days of old when he was King Thurindir's personal advisor as well as trusted friend.

"I know you're ready to go. I just came to wish you well and to ask the goddess to protect you on your journey and mission," he said gently, knowing I was close to losing it. "I know they're still alive, there's still time. Thea won't have given up hope you would come for her. Bring her back safely to us all," Talawen finished, pulling me into an embrace. Swallowing down a bucketload of emotion, I nodded, knowing only too well the need for this mission to be a success, not just for the kingdom but for me as well. I couldn't live without her.

Shaking my head to help me focus, I walked back to the other Thills who all stood ready to leave. Renad and his team came up at that moment and after a quick discussion with him, we left. There were twenty-four of us in total: ten Thanes, twelve Thills and Baylin and

Logan, who had fought their case as to why they should come. They had already begun to prove their worth as Thills in training and would be an asset to our team, but I just hoped they wouldn't let emotion get in the way of our purpose and do something foolish.

Lying in position, we were waiting about a mile south of the Waterfall of Knowledge. The information Caleb had received suggested the soldiers were going to attack here, waiting for some of the students to come out from training. Eyowel was going to make sure he walked out as part of a group, as we felt it would be more likely they would take a group, rather than trying to kidnap one Elf on their own.

It wasn't until dusk had settled that there was any movement. At first it looked like Minen's six guards were just innocent Elves making their way home, until they suddenly stopped, each taking position partially covered, near the waterfall. Our group were stationed further away so we would remain unseen.

Realising this was it, Taro released the bird that would give the signal to Eyowel to come out, and knowing he had to wait for the next group of students, we only had to sit in anticipation for a little while before we saw him walk out with about four others.

Renad and I decided that there was no way we could warn the students what was happening, as it was too much of a risk to their safety as they might accidently give something away. Instead, we made a vow that they would all be under our protection and would get out of this alive.

Seconds later the students and Eyowel were ambushed. They only had moments to register their surprise before one by one they were given a drug that must have knocked them out as they fell in quick succession to the ground. The guards then took one each, swinging them over their shoulders and quickly disappearing into the undergrowth.

Signalling to the others, we went into action, following about a hundred yards behind. The hostages were obviously still under the influence as they hung limply, arms swinging side to side as the soldiers ran at a fast pace. Knowing their destination made it easier to follow, but just in case we lost them, there were two Thanes at the base of the mountains who would tail them from there.

Eventually the towering mountains came into view and I could feel the others come alive like there was a spark in the air, in anticipation of what was to come. Keeping pace, it was pitch black before we came to a stop and I watched closely as the solider in front muttered a spell that caused a stone to roll away and an entrance to appear. Looking around first, they then went through and disappeared, followed closely by our two scouts who had waited up ahead.

Running forward, we stopped at the same place Minen's guards had, and Taro came to the front using his affinity to earth to also make the entrance reveal itself. Hurrying through, we were met by one of our scouts, who led us in the same direction as the hostages. The smell of damp, musty earth was all around us as we travelled further and further into the mountain. It would have been impossible to see if it hadn't been for the torches lining the way.

After running for fifty minutes at a steady pace, the temperature began to drop as we eventually made our way out into a large open cave that had stalagmites covering most of the floor. It must have been well below freezing, I observed, looking at the icy puddles around us. In another situation, this room would have been beautiful, as crystals sparkled, reflecting off our torches.

Coming to a stop Renad and the scout who had waited for us were having a heated conversation. Expecting the worst, I walked over to them to find out what the problem was.

"I don't know what to suggest, he should have been waiting for us by now, he and I agreed we'd only stay about twenty minutes away from each other at most and we haven't seen him for over an hour," the scout insisted, starting to get agitated.

Renad shot a meaningful look in my direction. We both knew that if the scout wasn't where he said he'd be, it was more than likely he'd been captured and that Minen knew we were here. However, before I could say a word, we were surrounded. Goblins, Ogres and Elves appeared, blocking the only two exits and therefore our escape. We were trapped.

Realising we were going to have to fight our way out, I took my usual stance, back to back with Eli, a sword in each hand ready for battle.

"For the queen," I shouted before they swarmed

towards us.

Looking to my right, an Ogre of monstrous proportions was headed straight for us, waving a club the length of a tree trunk in his hand. It was particularly grotesque. Standing about twelve feet tall, its facial features looked distorted as small beady eyes were set next to a huge deformed mouth that set in a snarl. Lumbering forwards, it swung at our heads just as I shouted at Eli to duck. Rolling forwards, I went between its legs and turned sharply, plunging my sword into its leg. Roaring in pain, it swung around trying to hit me like I was some pesky fly. Eli, who was now facing the Ogre's back, managed to climb up onto its shoulders as I then started to hack away at its front. Moments later Eli had thrust his dagger deep into the Ogre's head, trying to keep balance as it then stumbled around before finally crashing to the ground.

"One to me!" Eli smirked as straightaway he engaged in another battle, this time with a Goblin and two Elves.

"Ha! That only counted as a half! If I hadn't been there, you wouldn't have managed to get in that final blow!" I laughed back. Eli always got competitive at times like this.

About to join him, I halted, surrounded by my own set of Minen's soldiers. It was times like these that showed why I was Head Thill as I stabbed, punched and hit my way through them all in record speed. The mission, clearly at the forefront of my mind, was also incentive enough to come through this fight alive.

Taking a moment, I saw that Renad and Taro had also teamed up and, like Eli and I had, they were both slaughtering their way through a group of Elves and Goblins who had surrounded them. Going to offer my assistance, I met a particularly nasty looking Goblin who managed to kick me in the ribs before swiping his sword in a motion that was clearly supposed to take my head off. Thank goodness for my Elf abilities, which meant I was too quick for him. I went on the attack with renewed strength, picking him apart bit by bit as I cut off first one, then the other arm. Adopting an expression of disbelief as he realised what had happened, all he could do was hiss before I then cut off his head, feeling a sense of justice that another enemy had lost their life. The more the merrier, I felt, as I then looked around for someone else's life to end.

I was pleased to see the fight was pretty much over as the last few enemies were killed. Luckily we seemed to have come out of the battle fairly unscathed. Eli had a gash running down the length of his arm that he was wrapping cloth around, as it was seeping a steady stream of blood, and Baylin had a whopping swelling above his eye, but other than that, there were only a few minor scrapes and wounds.

Giving the others a few moments to collect themselves, we then continued into the only other exit. Hold on Thea, I thought to myself, as we ran forward with renewed determination. I'm coming.

TWENTY-FIVE

ESCAPE
THEA

It was becoming easier for me to channel spirit so that we could pass the guards unnoticed, especially as adrenaline was my newfound friend, fuelling my purpose. I did think that if the situation wasn't so dire, I could almost have fun with this newfound talent of mine.

We sneaked past the first guard without being discovered and after doing a quick reconnaissance, Inwen told me she had counted eighteen prisoners in total, with most doubled up in cells. The doors had bolts at the top and bottom that luckily Inwen was tall enough to reach, but even so, one squeaky door and it'd be history.

Both of us were half crawling, half knee-walking across the floor and tried our hardest to keep to the side when the guards patrolled the length of the room. Trying to focus on moving as well as getting my brain to keep sending spirit to all twelve guards was exhausting, and I had to keep stopping as after a while, even the adrenaline ran out and I felt permanently dizzy. This wasn't good as we still had another five cells to reach.

Inwen stood up, still making sure she had physical contact with me to maintain the spirit link between us, and slid the top bolt, followed by the one at the bottom of the next cell. With a quick look around to check the guards weren't looking directly at us, she then let go of me and gestured frantically to the female prisoner who must have been about twelve or thirteen at the most. At first she looked like she thought she'd gone mad, but the longer Inwen waved, the more responsive the girl became, coming out of her confused state and shuffling forward to hear what Inwen had to say. After a hurried conversation, the girl's eyes lit up with a renewed sense that she might live through this.

We got the same reaction from the next couple of cells and I wondered how many of them had already been experimented on. Most looked exhausted and their eyes flitted back and forth nervously, some wincing as they moved. Getting angrier and angrier, I shuddered in empathy at their pain, knowing that just like them, my elemental magic was a part of my very essence, my being, and I was damn sure Minen would pay for what he had done.

After the twelfth prisoner had been informed, I squeezed Inwen's hand to let her know I needed to rest. Beads of sweat had appeared on my forehead due to the strain I was putting myself under, and seeing Inwen's appearance flicker in front of me, I realised I soon wouldn't be able to control spirit at all.

After taking a moment, we continued on as the prisoners who had already received the message watched doors open and close as we made our way round to the final cells. Luckily the guards continued to remain unaware of what was going on; I guess they weren't really paying attention because it was so unlikely in their eyes the prisoners would try to escape.

It was at the last cell that I almost screamed at the horrifying scene that greeted us: Elder Erwin! I couldn't believe the change in his appearance, especially in such a short space of time. I mean, he had been fit and healthy at the coronation.

Erwin lay on his side, face beaten to a pulp, to the point where I almost didn't recognise him. He was moaning gently, clearly in his own world and unaware of his surroundings as he rocked back and forth. Clutching his stomach, he looked to be in a lot of pain and I wondered for a moment whether he would actually come out of this alive. It wasn't looking good, especially as Inwen and I weren't strong enough to carry him.

I could feel Inwen's hand shaking in mine and knew she had also recognised the councillor. Taking a deep breath to calm myself, I leaned over and whispered to her that we'd need to see if he was conscious enough to even recognise who we were and escape with us. I agreed to go in with her for support, and after opening the door cautiously, we took a few steps inside the cell. Immediately we were hit with the smell of rotten flesh and had to swallow down bile as we knew the smell was coming from Erwin.

"Elder Erwin...Elder Erwin, it's me, Thea," I said quietly, as I leaned down towards him. Tentatively I touched his shoulder, not wanting to cause him more pain. Not getting a response, I tried again. "Elder Erwin, can you hear me, it's Thea, we've come to rescue you!"

I pressed down more firmly onto his shoulder this time, trying again to get his attention, but the wail that came from him as a result caused me to fall backwards to the ground and I watched in horror as he continued to become more and more agitated. Oh goddess what had they done to him? I thought, staring in disbelief at this man who had previously been so strong and charismatic.

"We can't do anything," Inwen whispered to me, realising I was struggling to keep it together. "Come on...we need to keep going, we're going to have to leave him here."

Feeling numb and slightly disoriented, I let her pull me out of the cell as she closed the door behind us. We'd finished stage one, I thought, as the other prisoners moved slowly towards their doors, ready for the next part in our escape plan. This was the part when I was going to blind the guards, whilst those who could, including Inwen, would use their own element or even just brute strength to force them into the cells. The doors would then be locked so they had no means of escaping. The problem was I knew I had already used up almost all of my strength and was running on empty. Sagging, I dropped to the floor, trying at least to stay upright as black spots crept into my vision. Seeing I was spent, Inwen knelt down next to me, still holding on to my hand.

"You can do this Thea, I believe in you, you have to

keep going. We're almost there."

"I can't...I'm exhausted...it's too much; I can't do this anymore," I replied, shaking my head. The picture of Elder Erwin kept replaying in my head and I couldn't stop thinking that it could have been me lying there in a bloody mess if my extraction had worked. I was sick of being the strong leader everyone expected me to be. I mean, I was still only seventeen years old! This was wrong on so many levels and I began sobbing quietly, not bothering to brush away the tears that were streaming down my face.

"No Thea, you can't do this. Don't break down. I need you. We all need you...look around you!" she said, her voice wobbling as she tried to hold her emotion in and remain strong, even though she was just as exhausted as I was.

Looking up I saw what she meant as eighteen pairs of eyes, including Kayla's, stared expectantly, almost desperately at me. Asking the goddess for strength, I felt a surge of warmth and knew that although I couldn't see her, she was here with me. I couldn't give up on them. Whatever I was feeling, they were my subjects and I needed to lead them like a queen would.

Rubbing my hands across my face I prepared myself, ready to change the guards' vision so that instead of our invisibility, they would now experience blindness.

"Now!" I shouted at the exact moment I knew they were unable to see. It was so satisfying to witness as all twelve guards thrashed around, unable to see what was going on whilst prisoners escaped their cells, using magic or any other means possible to trap their captors into the now empty cages. Standing up, I moved forward to help the others when my vision suddenly went and I toppled over as another wave of dizziness hit. Swearing loudly, I managed to stand back up and looked around to see my fears were becoming reality. The guards could see again and were beginning to fight back.

A feeling of dread hit me, knowing this was going to end badly if I couldn't find the strength to blind them again. There was no other way the prisoners were going to overcome the guards, even though there were more of them. Many had little strength, clearly having been starved for days, whilst others were young and completely inexperienced at fighting.

"Thea!" Inwen yelled as I turned towards her to see what was wrong now. I was too slow as in the next second I was hit from behind, someone using a weapon that felt like a sledgehammer to my head. Turning round I saw one of the guards was inches from my face as he grabbed hold of my shoulders, throwing me to the ground. Refusing to give up, I pushed my hands out in front of me and used air to throw him back into the wall behind him. I then stood up, quickly taking up a defensive stance, trying to ignore the egg-shaped bump on the back of my head that was still swelling. A nasty headache was also pounding in rhythm with my heartbeat.

Just then the guard lunged forward as I brought up my leg to kick him in the stomach. Before I had a chance to make contact, another guard had joined in our fight and grabbed my arm, yanking it back painfully behind my back. Struggling to get free, I kicked out at his legs as he swung me around, smacking my head on the wall. I swore loudly as I could feel the blood trickling down the side of my face.

Somehow I managed to get back up and glanced

around at the chaotic scene in front of me as prisoners continued fighting when an ear-splitting siren went off. Oh goddess, no! The guards had alerted the others to our breakout.

The screeching noise actually seemed to spur the prisoners on, as we became more desperate knowing our window for escape was closing. Inwen and the girl from the first cell we had opened were holding their own against a guard at least twice their size, but I then had to focus on my own problems as I watched two Goblins stalk towards me. I didn't have too long to prepare myself as they both suddenly charged, one waving a sword that was enormous. Realising the only thing I could do was duck, I did so and put my hands out, ready to blast them to one side, but I was too late. While the one with the sword got side-tracked by another prisoner who had come to my aid, the first Goblin elbowed me heavily in the chest and then flipped me over backwards so I smacked into the floor.

This time I couldn't hold back the scream that came from me. The pain was immense and I was sure he had cracked my ribs as well as possibly my wrist due to the funny way I had landed. Cradling my arm, I refused to be beaten or show any weakness, and rolled over, staring defiantly at him. If this was my end, then I wanted to die staying strong.

Slowly I got back up as he watched me struggle. His face was in an ugly sneer, and spittle mixed with his blood dripped off his face. He didn't look in a hurry to finish me off and smirked as my breaths came out in short gasps, another sign that I didn't have long left. Taking one last glance around, I sent a prayer to the goddess that she would somehow get Inwen and Kayla out alive and then stood up straighter, ignoring the constant throb and waves of pain that were all over my body now.

Just then, when I thought all was lost, I saw him: Isaac. He was standing by the entrance, staring at me with a horrified look on his face as Thills and Thanes streamed past him, including my beloved Eli, Caleb and Taro, who were all ready for battle. If this was a dream, or I had now become delirious, that was fine by me. I was happy never to wake up again as my heart swelled to bursting point seeing him standing only about twenty feet away. Isaac had found me. My protector, my love had done it. The prisoners were saved and I smiled trying to reassure him I was okay.

However, as I continued to look his way, even in my hazy state I became confused. Why wasn't he happy? He had made it. We were going to get through this. If anything his face was looking more and more tortured if his look of anguish was anything to go by. He started forward, mouthing something desperately at me, but I couldn't understand what was wrong. Looking around for a clue, I suddenly found the answer. Distracted by Isaac's entrance, the Goblin that had attacked me was obviously ready to finish me off. Not put off by the new wave of Thills and Thanes trying to attack the rest of Minen's army, he stalked forward, pursuing me with renewed vigour until at the last moment he lunged forward, sword in hand. Aimed at my stomach, it made contact as he thrust through into my flesh, twisting at the last second to cause even more pain.

As though time were slowing down, I looked down in astonishment. How had I let this happen? "No!" I whispered as I searched for Isaac again in the sea of men. The torment on his face was heart-breaking as he realised he was too late. He was still too far away.

Ignoring everything else, and knowing I was too exhausted to fight back anymore, I had eyes only for Isaac, trying to show him in that moment how much he meant to me.

"I love you," I mouthed at him, knowing I wouldn't get another chance.

Ready for the inevitable, I closed my eyes, knowing my attacker's next move would mean my certain death.

TWENTY-SIX

MY GUARDIAN ANGEL

Seconds had passed and nothing had happened. I opened my eyes as I heard, to my utter astonishment, the Goblin screaming out in agony, clutching his head as he fell to the floor. As he rolled over I saw blood streaming out of his eyes, ears and mouth. In fact there was so much blood he looked like he was choking on it. Looking around, I wondered where this new threat was coming from, just as Isaac finally reached me, jumping over dead bodies in his haste. His face looked lethal as with deadly precision he focused on my attacker and, grabbing his sword, cut off his head.

Turning to face me, he was breathing rapidly as he searched my body, assessing my injuries. I tentatively put out my uninjured arm, wanting to touch him and check he really was here and that this was real. Finally grabbing a hold of him, I gasped as the pain in my stomach intensified, causing me to double over and slump to the floor. Tears leaked down my face as so many emotions seemed to go through me at once, but in that moment, even with all the pain I was feeling, knowing I was safe once again with my beloved became the predominant emotion.

"Thea," he said simply, as he gently laid me down and kissed my tears, eyes and then lips. "You are my life, the centre of my world. I love you."

"And I you," I murmured, knowing he could hear me even with the noise of all the fighting in the background.

Looking around him, Isaac hovered over me protectively in case there were any other nearby threats. However, it wasn't necessary as most of the fighting was now coming to an end. From what I could see, we had some casualties but it was Minen's side that had come off worse, I observed, looking at all the dead bodies littered around the room.

"Thea!" I heard someone shouting.

Pushing Isaac away, I chocked back a sob realising it was Eli, who had a small Kayla-shaped bundle attached to his side. The relief on his face at seeing us both safe and sound was tumultuous. He knelt down next to me, kissing my lips with a mischievous glint in his eye.

"Thank the goddess you're both alive!" he exclaimed, ignoring Isaac's growl. "And you've found the prisoners! Are you okay?" he finished worriedly, as he then took a proper look at me.

"Yes, I'm fine…we just need to get out of here," I insisted, trying once again to move against Isaac's hold on me and get up. Bad idea. Hissing, I sank back down to the floor, as any movement caused the pain in my stomach to become agonising.

"Shit, what are we going to do?" Eli asked, glancing at Isaac. He knew just like the rest of us we didn't have long before the rest of Minen's army would come looking for us.

Gasping, I tried to smile reassuringly at Kayla who looked terrified. "I'll be fine. Isaac, can you carry me? I don't have the energy to heal myself, I'll have to see a healer when I get out of this hell hole."

"Thea, I can't move you, there's too much blood, you need to be healed now," he started as he then proceeded to rip the hole in my dress until it was big enough for him to see the extent of my injury. Watching on in disbelief, he then put both his hands over my wound and closed his eyes in concentration. Eli and I gave each other a questioning look as a warm feeling in my stomach continued to grow. This couldn't be happening. Isaac could heal? He had an affinity to spirit?!

As he finished, rocking back on his heels, he gave us both a look of chagrin.

"I guess I've got something to tell you. You see, I've always had an affinity to spirit, but this is the first time I've actually been able to heal someone; I guess you were the incentive I needed!" He smirked, quirking his eyebrow at me.

"Well if there ever was a time to start being even more amazing than you already are, now would be it!" I smirked back, kissing him on the lips as Eli laughed.

Feeling my energy levels steadily returning, I realised most of my aches and pains had gone, and even though Isaac hadn't particularly focused on my wrist, the throb was now just a dull ache.

I stood up slowly, Isaac letting me lean on him, and re-assessed the scene before me. There were about nineteen Thills and Thanes standing quietly nearby, including my gorgeous near guards – Taro and Caleb as well as Baylin and Logan – all waiting for orders. Taro winked at me whilst Bay and Logan both had arms around an exhausted yet happy Inwen. Some were assisting the prisoners that had survived. I also saw that the Thane – Solan – and another were carrying an unconscious Elder Erwin between them.

Renad walked over at this point and greeted me, placing his fist on his chest.

"Thea-Driel, my queen, thank the goddess you're well. We have all been so worried."

Then he turned to Isaac. "What plans do you have for our escape?" he asked, as he and the others listened on expectantly to what he had to say.

TWENTY-SEVEN

BACK TO NORMALITY...IS THERE SUCH A THING?

As we ran back through the tunnels, progress was slow due to all of those who had significant injuries. There was no time to try heal everyone now, there were just too many, and the thought that at any moment Minen and his army would find us had put me on edge. The incessant sirens continued, but other than that all seemed suspiciously quiet. Even the torture chambers we ran past were devoid of any doctors or lifeless patients. It was like everyone had completely vanished.

When we made it back outside of the mountain, again no one tried to stop us. Climbing up on Terin, the anxiety I was feeling was ready to bubble over and I turned to look back at Isaac who sat behind me.

"Where do you think they are?" I whispered agitatedly, as paranoia set in. "I mean, I'm not complaining, but this doesn't feel right, something is off. What's Minen doing?"

"I don't know," he replied, looking just as concerned. "Our guards are prepared for further battle though, so don't worry, but I have to say that as long as we're getting closer to the palace and certain freedom I'm not going to question it.

It was then that Isaac took a good look at me and obviously saw something in my expression that made him concerned, as worry filled his eyes. Turning me fully so that I was now sat in his lap, one of his hands gently caressed the side of my face. Leaning down he kissed me gently on the lips. "Rest now Thea, it won't be long until we're back," he said soothingly as he spurred Terin on. Looking around me one last time, I was reassured to see that Inwen sat with Logan on his horse while Eli, Kayla, Bay and the other Thills also had horses and would be riding back with us in the first party. As there weren't enough horses for everyone, the second group led by Renad would be returning by foot until further aid could be sent to them.

As we set off, I tried to reassure myself that everything would be okay. The problem was, though, my recent captivity had left me feeling like I now knew Minen better than anyone. He definitely had something planned. We just had to find out what, and when he would strike, I thought, before succumbing to the gentle rocking motion and falling asleep.

I didn't have to wait long to find out.

"Oh Thea!" a voice called out, trying to take me away from the peaceful slumber I had found at last. "Thea, oh

Thea, open your eyes," the voice commanded, sounding more insistent this time.

Confused, I sat up, surprised I was no longer sat with Isaac on Terin, but instead sitting by the Waterfall of Knowledge. It was night and everything seemed to have a hazy aura around it.

"Fascinating isn't it? What the mind can do? How when we relax enough another can invade your dreams, which is how I can be here with you now!" the voice whispered behind me.

Turning suddenly I saw him, Minen, standing right in front of me with a delighted expression plastered on his face before he continued. "Judging by how you are now asleep, I'm guessing you managed to escape and are on your way home, which of course is what I planned for you to do. You may think you have won by rescuing the prisoners, but I have many more. You see this isn't my only hide-away, there are others filled with Elves and other species, all more or less willing to help me with my cause.

"I'm not giving up Thea, this is just the beginning. I just needed a little more time, which is why I let you go for now, and then I will find you and finish what I've started. I will build my master race, become Lord of all Faey and the rest of the world. I know what to do now, it was simply a matter of how we extracted the element that was holding us back. You helped us to see that, Thea, when we tried to take your magic. Thank you Thea, you are the reason I have now succeeded. We have a host, you see!" His eyes glinted at this point. "This host is just like you, able to wield all the elements, but stronger. He is the first of many! Soon I'll be coming for you Thea, soon!"

Waking with a start, I clutched my hands in front of me as though they were now my only lifeline, while a new kind of terror swept through me.

"He came to me in a dream," I whispered, not

wanting to say it out loud and make it even more real. Feeling Isaac tense behind me, I knew he had heard.

"Minen, he was there…it was him…it was real…he was inside my mind. He's coming… he has these plans, it's not just us, none of us are safe, oh goddess!" I gasped before huge wracking sobs escaped me. It was then my shaking became so severe, Isaac had to stop just so he could get a proper hold of me before I fell off Terin.

"Sshh, it's going to be okay. He won't get you, I'm never leaving you alone again. I'll kill Minen if he even dares to try," Isaac murmured gently, squeezing me even tighter to him as though that would help keep the ghosts at bay, but I continued sobbing, knowing it wouldn't.

As he gently rocked me, I knew soon I'd have to tell them all what Minen had planned, knowing how it would affect us all, not just the Elven race. If we didn't stop him soon, his evil would spread through the whole of Faery and the rest of the supernatural and human world as well. No one was safe from his maniacal ways. And who was going to go up against him? Me? At that thought a whole new round of fear coursed through me; it had to be me, I was the queen and he was my responsibility. It didn't matter that I was just a seventeen-year-old girl. Hell, it was only just over four months ago I had found out I was Faey.

As we journeyed on again, I knew any further sleep was now out of the question. Maybe the fear of the known is actually greater than that of the unknown? Curling in on myself whilst trying desperately to feel Isaac's warmth, I struggled to ignore the images of torture and destruction that seemed to be burnt into my retinas and my very existence.

Realising I was still awake, Isaac attempted to distract me as he began to fill me in on his plot for our rescue. He explained that Inwen and I had been missing for about eight nights, but to me it had felt much longer than that, an eternity I never wanted to relive. I wasn't quite sure how I or the other prisoners were going to get over the ordeal we had been through, but knew that at least we were safe for now.

Arriving back at the palace, we were greeted by many relieved looking faces, including that of a kindly looking brown-haired Elf who had eyes only for me. As Isaac lowered me gently off Terin, I hobbled as quickly as I could over to Talawen who swept me up in an all-consuming hug. I considered him a father figure just as much as I knew he saw me as a daughter, and it was a while before we broke apart.

"My queen, I am glad to see you are well. We have prayed to the goddess for your safe return and here you are! Your people will be glad to know you're back. Things have been... a little tense while you've been gone, especially with the turmoil Minen had left behind."

"It is good to see you too, Talawen, although I have something to tell you all: Minen...he left me a message," I started, feeling renewed strength as Isaac came and stood directly behind me, letting me lean into him for support. As the others came to join us, having already greeted their loved ones, I led them inside where I recounted my dream and all it entailed.

It had been two weeks since I'd returned and Aroben was getting back to some sort of normality. I was even beginning to take over the running of the kingdom – with Talawen's help of course. The nation now knew Minen was behind the kidnappings and many were outraged with his insane ideals – to make a super race over which he would rule. We obviously hadn't shared the full extent of what Minen had planned with the general population, as it would just create further panic. However, a select few knew the whole truth. These included representatives on the Faey Council as well as kings and queens from around Faey, many of whom had experienced the recent events first hand at my coronation and knew what he was capable of. As a result of all our growing concerns, a meeting had been scheduled for a month's time in Maesdra, Queen Syndra's kingdom, to address how we were going to overcome the threat Faey was now facing. All twelve species would be attending as well as dignitaries from further afield, and knowing those present would be looking to me for direction was a particular burden I was finding difficult to bear, not that I was going to share that with anyone, however much I wanted to. My people needed me to be strong. I just had to keep going somehow.

Minen hadn't come to me again in a dream since the night we escaped, thank the goddess. Talawen explained that Minen's ability to dream-weave was a very rare gift and one he had not shared with anyone. Luckily though, he explained I could shield my mind from any further attack and that was something we'd been working on daily since I'd returned. The key was to not let my mental barriers down, especially if I became emotionally or physically drained. Fortunately, being a spirit user was particularly advantageous in keeping up these blocks, which was a relief as I did not want to experience that again.

Isaac had been like my shadow along with Eli, Inwen, Bay, Logan and the Thills, all of whom I now considered my family. I had my suspicions that Isaac was making sure I wasn't left on my own for too long, as he continued to see the effect recent events had had on me – everyone could see I was exhausted from lack of sleep, but Isaac got an even greater insight as he was the one having to console me night after night when he woke up to my screaming. The dreams filled with death and destruction had taken their toll on both of us.

Which brings me back to this day, and why I was standing dressed all in black. It appears the custom of wearing black to a funeral is the same here as in the human realm. The day I'd been dreading, Janin's funeral, was finally here. Being a Thill guard, he would have a public ceremony and hundreds were expected to attend.

Sighing deeply, I looked again in the mirror at the woman I'd become. The queen who so many were relying on – the queen who so many had already lost their lives for. Clutching my robe, I turned to walk towards my bedroom door as a gentle knock sounded. I opened it to see not only Isaac, but my family, all crowding round to hug me and give me looks of warmth and support. This day would be hard for all of us, but it was a day we also needed to remember. Today was a time to celebrate Janin's life and not only reflect on what an amazing guard he had been, but also to remember the reason for his death – to ensure others had their freedom.

Walking in tight formation, we headed outside and down to Lake Fallowen where the funeral was to be held, as this was one of Janin's favourite places. Willow trees blew gently in the wind and it felt like the branches were bowing down in respect. White lilies had been scattered along the path down to the ceremony, and once there I saw how packed with Faey the area had already become, a credit to how much Janin had been loved.

Recent events had meant security had been increased tenfold, and as it was a Thill guard that had died, it was the Thanes who helped with the security while the Thills took their positions at the ends of each row as a sign of respect.

Starting from the back row, I made my way down the aisle with Isaac as Head Thill directly behind me. The procession was a slow one and ended with us being greeted by Janin's parents, who were seated up in the front row. As they wept silently at the tragic loss of their son, the guilt I felt knowing he had given up his life to protect me gnawed away at me. I went to hug them fiercely, hoping they'd realise how thankful I was he had been a part of my life. I would make it up to them somehow, even if I had to kill Minen myself.

The ceremony was beautiful, led by Talawen. He and the other Elders had seats on a raised platform at the front, although there were a few noticeable absences – Minen obviously, but also Elder Lhinanor, who had been declared missing since the night of my coronation. Both had yet to be replaced. Callon had also disappeared, but I wondered if he had gone with his father or had run away. Either way I felt like it wasn't the last I'd see of that family.

A couple of hours later most of the congregation

had dispersed. Taking a moment to myself, I walked off towards the Forest of Arlain with a couple of Thills – Isaac not too far behind. Leaning against a tree, I shut my eyes, breathing in deeply the heavenly scent of nature surrounding me.

"This is one of my thinking spots too," a voice spoke, starling me.

Standing up, I started to move into a defensive stance and then stopped. I knew who this was, not just from the countless paintings I had seen of her, but from the aura of love she projected.

"Goddess Elebrin, it is an honour to meet you!" I exclaimed, bowing before her.

"Please Thea, there's no need to bow. It is I who am honoured to meet you. I am so proud of what you have achieved in such a short space of time. I know your parents would be proud; it was I who told your mother the role you would play in changing our world for the betterment of all."

I could only stare in awe as a golden hue seemed to emanate around her.

"I came today to give you courage child...your journey has only just begun, and whilst you will continue to face hardships along the way, know that I will always be with you," she said, as she held out her hand to put something in mine. Looking down, I realised it was a necklace made out of a white crystal with tiny diamonds around the edge.

"This necklace contains my light, my peace and my love for when you need it most," she said, before turning to walk away. Watching her go, it wasn't long before she faded into the nature surrounding her. Blinking, I wondered what had just happened. If I didn't have the necklace as evidence, I would have thought I'd lost my mind.

"Thea," Isaac called out gently, not wanting to startle me further.

"Did you see...?" I started, as he just nodded in response, a look of awe on his face too.

Putting on the necklace, I took his hand and walked back to the rest of my near guard who had also been joined by the others – Taro, Caleb, Eli, Bay, Inwen and Logan.

"The time has come," I began, looking round at them all.

"We must fight, we must remember what we feel here today as a result of Janin's death. We will go to meet with the Faey Council and continue on this journey we have begun, into further battle if we must. Minen will not win and we are the ones to stop him," I finished resolutely before walking back to the palace, the others in tow.

I just hoped I could keep my promise.

ABOUT THE AUTHOR

I live in Surrey, England, a short walk from the beautiful Windsor Park, with my husband Richard and our two children Noah and Olivia.

For me, writing is nothing short of an addiction and I often find myself sneaking out to my writing shed for just a few minutes, which can often turn into hours of pure, unadulterated bliss catching up with my characters and continuing their story. Although I'm currently writing the third book in the Driel trilogy, other characters involving all things fantasy, paranormal and YA romance are jockeying for position, wanting me to write their story next, so watch this space!

It is such a privilege to share my stories with you the reader and I always love to hear from you so please get in contact using the links below:

Website: www.lizkeelauthor.com
Facebook: www.facebook.com/lizkeelauthor
Twitter: @lizkeelauthor